Praise for Brian Gallagher's books:

Across the Divide

'The atmosphere of a troubled city awash with tension and poverty is excellently captured' *Irish Examiner*

'A compelling historical novel' *Inis Magazine*

'Highly recommended' *Bookfest*

Taking Sides

'An involving, exciting read … a first class adventure' *Carousel Magazine*

'Gripping right from its first page…dramatic action and storytelling skill' *Evening Echo*

'Riveting' *Sunday Independent*

Secrets and Shadows

'Story of friendship and suspicion, excitement and intrigue' *The Scotsman*

'Heart-stopping action likely to hold readers aged nine to teens in its thrall' *Evening Echo*

'deftly weaving historic fact and period detail into a fictional but nevertheless entirely credible story … nail-biting' *Books Ireland*

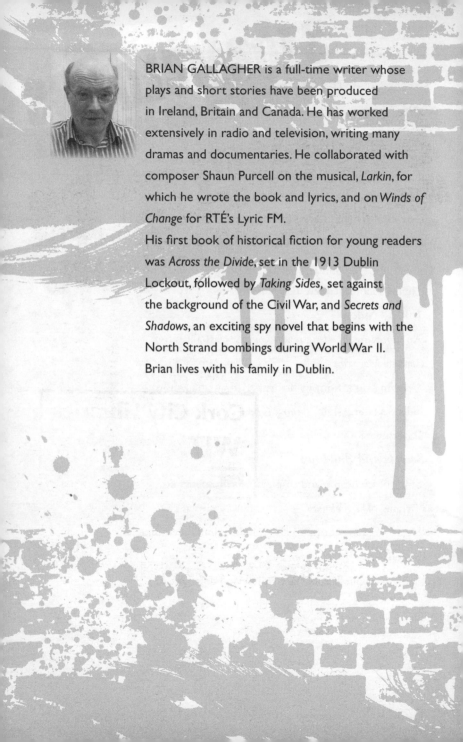

BRIAN GALLAGHER is a full-time writer whose plays and short stories have been produced in Ireland, Britain and Canada. He has worked extensively in radio and television, writing many dramas and documentaries. He collaborated with composer Shaun Purcell on the musical, *Larkin*, for which he wrote the book and lyrics, and on *Winds of Change* for RTÉ's Lyric FM.

His first book of historical fiction for young readers was *Across the Divide*, set in the 1913 Dublin Lockout, followed by *Taking Sides*, set against the background of the Civil War, and *Secrets and Shadows*, an exciting spy novel that begins with the North Strand bombings during World War II. Brian lives with his family in Dublin.

DEDICATION

To my aunts, Joan and Pat, the matriarchs of our family.

ACKNOWLEDGEMENTS

My sincere thanks to Michael O'Brien for his suggestion of a children's novel set against the backdrop of the Northern Troubles, to my editor, Mary Webb, for her usual skilful editing and advice, to publicist Ruth Heneghan for all her efforts on my behalf, to Emma Byrne for her sterling work on cover design, and to everyone at The O'Brien Press, with whom, as ever, it's a pleasure to work.

I'm grateful to Cliona Fitzsimons for her support, and to Connor Kelly, Emer Geisser and Ciara Fitzsimons, three young readers who shared with me their views of an early draft of the story.

My thanks also go to Hugh McCusker for his painstaking proof-reading, to Ken and Maureen Eccles, and Keith and Jane Adams for sharing their childhood memories of Belfast, to Jim Rodgers and Joan Eccles for help with maps of the period, and to Anne Maxwell for allowing me access to archive material in the Falls Road Library. The subject matter of this book is still sensitive for many people, and any errors, artistic licence or opinions expressed are mine and mine alone.

And finally, the greatest thanks of all go to my family, Miriam, Orla and Peter, for their unflagging support.

PROLOGUE:

15 AUGUST 1969
BOMBAY STREET, BELFAST, NORTHERN IRELAND

Maeve wanted to scream. Instead she forced herself to make no sound. Determined not to reveal her whereabouts, she bit her lip and crouched back against the wall of her hiding place. She could hear the roaring mob outside on her street, and she tried to make herself even smaller as she hid in the dark cupboard space under the living room stairs, praying that they wouldn't find her.

The trouble that had been brewing in Belfast for months had finally erupted and now people from neighbouring districts were violently attacking each other. The air was rent with gunfire, screams, the smashing of glass and the roar of flames as house after house was set on fire. Maeve knew from the news on the radio that much of the city had turned into a war zone. It meant that she couldn't count on the police to rescue her, and so she was trapped here alone, with no one to help her.

Even though she was more frightened than she had ever been in her life, she was angry too. Why did people have to be so horrible and cruel to one another? Maeve had been living with her aunt and uncle in Belfast for three years now, but she still found it hard to understand why so many Catholics and Protestants hated each other. Her Uncle Jim said Catholic nationalists like themselves were a minority in Northern Ireland, where most people were Protestant loyalists – who wanted to stay in the United Kingdom. Uncle Jim said nationalists mostly wanted a united Ireland, though in the meantime lots of them would settle for a fair deal on decent jobs and houses.

But it was one thing for Uncle Jim to explain how people felt, another to deal with the hatred that had erupted in the last two days. And just when she needed him most, her uncle was away working in Donegal. Aunt Nan hadn't been able to get home either, and was now trapped in the Ardoyne district, a small nationalist area that was also under siege. Aunt Nan had gone there to visit a sick friend, only to find herself unable to get safely out again. She had sent a message to Maeve, via a neighbour who had a telephone, and had insisted that Maeve was to lock the front door and stay put, and under no circumstance to go out onto Bombay Street.

As if I'd want to, Maeve had thought irritably. Being twelve years old she found it annoying when her aunt treated her like a baby – though just now she would have happily curled up in the comfort of Aunt Nan's arms. Thinking of her aunt, Maeve began feeling tearful. No! she told herself, getting weepy wasn't going to solve anything. She had to keep her wits about her and fend for herself.

The gunfire and noise from the streets outside were getting even louder, and Maeve was glad that she had resisted the temptation to make a run for the nearby Clonard Monastery. It was a big building in its own grounds, and its basement had been used as a community air raid shelter during the Second World War. But the mob swarming through the streets was so crazed now that Maeve feared they wouldn't see the Catholic monastery as a refuge to be respected, but might well see it as a target.

Suddenly there was a loud thud from nearby, and Maeve started in shock. The sound came again and she realised that someone was pounding on the front door. Oh God, she thought, please, let the lock hold!

The banging got louder, and Maeve bit her lip again. There was more banging, then a splintering sound, followed by the hall door being smashed against the wall. Maeve felt her heart pounding madly. She prayed that whoever had broken in wouldn't think of looking into the small, dark storage space under the stairs.

She held her breath as several people came clattering into the living room. There was loud laughter and whooping as the rioters violently overturned tables and chairs and smashed ornaments in the living room and adjoining kitchenette. Maeve felt sickened at the destruction, knowing how house-proud Aunt Nan was. Even as she thought it, however, part of her brain realised that none of that really mattered. Tables and chairs could be replaced. But if they found her hiding place there was no telling what might happen.

Before she could worry any further she heard a harsh, drunken voice. It was startlingly close – just on the other side of the wooden door that separated under the stairs from the living room – and the man's words were horrifying.

'Take that can and douse upstairs, Davy! We'll do here!'

Maeve felt a stab of panic, even though she had known that the house might be set on fire.

'My pleasure!' answered the man with a drunken laugh, 'my pleasure!'

'And don't skimp with the petrol, Davy!' the first man cried, laughing as though it were all a great joke. 'We don't want the Taigs saying we short-changed them!'

Maeve heard the man called Davy pounding up the stairs that ran over her head, then the rioters in the front room gave another whoop of triumph. Maeve realised that they had found the money that Aunt Nan kept in a tin on the mantelpiece. She heard them arguing over how to split it, and she willed them to continue their drunken dispute, hoping that it would distract them from opening the door to her hiding place.

She heard more footsteps as someone else entered the room. The new man spoke. His voice was cold and hard and somehow more frightening for not sounding drunk like the others.

'Any Taigs here?' he asked.

'Taigs' was an insulting word for nationalists or Catholics, and Maeve felt her legs trembling at the thought of this man finding her. She wrapped her hands around her knees to keep them still.

'Not down here,' answered the first rioter. 'Davy's checking upstairs.'

There was a pause, and Maeve imagined the new arrival noticing the door under the stairs and yanking it open. She held her breath, desperately anxious to do nothing to alert him to her presence.

'OK, torch the place,' said the new man.

Maeve felt her mouth go dry but she forced herself not to panic. She had read an adventure story in which the heroine survived a fire by using buckets of water and a wet blanket to protect herself. Copying the girl from the story, Maeve had filled several buckets of water earlier and taken a blanket off her bed. Her hope was that even if the house was set on fire the stone walls wouldn't collapse. If she could protect herself long enough with the wet blanket the rioters might pass through her neighbourhood, allowing her to emerge eventually.

It was a frightening plan, but before she could think about it any more she heard a shout from the front room. 'Let's go, Davy!' There was a sudden whoosh as the petrol-doused room was set ablaze. Maeve cowered against the back wall, feeling the heat through the thin partition that separated her from the burning room. The man called Davy must have set the bedrooms alight also, because there was another whoosh of flames from above, then the man shrieked with delight and pounded down the stairs.

'That will warm their hearts!' cried the first drunken rioter, kicking a chair against the wall in farewell as he made his way towards the hall door.

Maeve felt a flood of relief that the men had left without finding her. The relief didn't last for long, though. The rioters had left her house, but there was still mayhem outside. And in here the blaze was taking hold. Maeve could feel the heat coming down from the upper floor, and she quickly soaked the blanket in the first bucket of water, then wrapped it around herself. The cold, wet blanket felt horrible against her skin, but it could save her life, and she wet herself thoroughly, trying to ignore the terrifying crackle of the fire from the living room.

Smoke was now coming in through the cracks in the cupboard door, and Maeve coughed, then pulled the wet blanket around her mouth and nose. She had originally thought that the rioters would use only petrol bombs to damage the house. She realised now that in dousing the individual rooms with petrol they had started a more serious fire. And if it continued spreading, the wooden partition wall between under the stairs and the living room would eventually go up in flames, exposing her to the full blast of the fire. But if she tried to make a run for it she risked not only the flames, but also discovery by the rioters – to say nothing of the shooting and fighting that was going on outside.

Moving forward in the darkened space, she splashed water from the second bucket onto the inside of the cupboard wall. The smoke was getting worse now, and she found herself coughing again. Despite being wrapped in the wet blanket it was getting uncomfortably hot. She got another fit of coughing and began to wonder if she wasn't making a terrible mistake. Supposing the fire didn't burn itself out? Supposing it spread and burnt everything in the house to a cinder? She could hear the sound of the two upstairs bedrooms blazing now and she was racked with indecision. Stay, and hope to escape the rioters, but maybe get burnt alive? Or risk running through the blazing room and then taking her chances out on the battlefield that was her neighbourhood?

She hesitated, wishing there was someone to help her. 'Pray to Our Lady for guidance,' Aunt Nan always said, and in desperation Maeve now prayed for help. No sooner had she finished a quick prayer, however, than she got another, worse, bout of choking from the thickening smoke. The rasping coughing hurt her lungs, and it didn't seem like her prayer had been answered. But maybe it had, she thought. Maybe this was a signal that she shouldn't stay here.

Still she hesitated, terrified to face the blaze. But the darkened cupboard became hotter and brighter, as tongues of flame began to lick the door and outer wall. She couldn't stay here. She was going to die, unless she got up the nerve to brave both the flames and the battle outside.

Her mind suddenly made up, she doused the blanket again with water. She wrapped it around herself, then took the second pail and upended it over her head, so that she was soaked. She paused briefly, getting her nerve up. Then she steeled herself, drew the blanket up over her head, and pulled open the door to the blazing living room.

PART ONE

ENCOUNTERS

CHAPTER ONE

MARCH 1969

WANDERERS SOCCER CLUB, BELFAST.

Dylan wished his mother was less of a hippy. He loved her, of course, but there was a time for being arty and a time for being normal. And right now, when he was being dropped off to football training with his friend Sammy, he wished Mom would be a bit more normal. Instead she was singing along to the car radio as she drove up to the sports ground in her new Ford Granada

The song was her latest favourite, 'Where do you go to my Lovely' and, sitting in the back seat with Sammy, Dylan felt slightly embarrassed. Dylan had met Sammy's mother – a Belfast woman who worked long hours in a mill – and he couldn't imagine her singing along soulfully to Peter Sarstedt's hit song the way his own mother was.

'This will do us, Mom,' he said as they drew up to the entrance to the sports ground.

'It's OK, I'll drive right in.'

'There's no need.'

'Relax, Dylan, it's cool.'

But it wasn't cool, Dylan thought, as his mother drove confidently in through the entrance gate. Her flashy wine-coloured Granada simply highlighted how Dylan came from a different type of family to the other twelve-year-old boys on the team. If he hadn't been friends with Sammy, who was admired as the best full back in the club, he would have felt even more of an odd-man-out.

He raised an eyebrow now to Sammy, who gave him a wry, sympathetic grin. It was good to have a friend who was normal, though it also brought home to Dylan how much he himself was different. In the overwhelmingly Christian city of Belfast, Dylan, his twin sister Emma, and his father were Jewish. Not very religious Jews, but still Jewish, and therefore different. Blond, tanned, Jewish, from America – everything about them had seemed at odds with the locals when Dad had been posted to Belfast a couple of months ago. Dylan and Emma had been born in Leeds, however, and during the four years that they had spent in America they were known as the English kids. But now they spoke and thought like Americans, so they wouldn't have fitted in back in Leeds either.

Even though Dylan's family had an enjoyable lifestyle and had rented a big, comfortable house on the Malone Road, he still envied Sammy in some ways. Sammy lived in a much smaller terraced house off Tate's Avenue. It was a modest two-bedroomed redbrick home like countless others in Belfast, and unlike himself and Emma, Sammy wouldn't have to make any effort to fit in, he would be just like all of his friends and neighbours.

'OK, honey, play well,' said Dylan's mother now as the car came to a halt.

'Thanks, Mom, see you later,' he answered, opening the rear door and quickly nodding farewell, in case his mother tried to kiss him goodbye in front of the other players.

'Thanks for the lift, Mrs Goldman,' said Sammy.

'You're welcome, Sammy. Score a hat trick!'

'He's a full back, Mom,' said Dylan.

'Well, then … do what full backs do!'

His mother grinned, revved the engine, then beeped the horn in farewell and drove off. It was typical of Mom, Dylan thought. She was totally at ease with herself and felt that she fitted in everywhere – even when she didn't. Mom really was American, and came from a rich family that had lived for generations on Long Island, outside New York City. She had the confidence that came from money and status, and Dad sometimes laughingly called her a WASP, which Dylan knew stood for White, Anglo-Saxon Protestant. Not that Mom was very religious. And nobody in the family took seriously her recent dabbling in Buddhism, least of all Dylan, who thought this was just more of Mom wanting to be a hippy. Which was OK for his mother, but made him and Emma targets for jokes and snide comments.

As the Granada drove off, he turned away, carrying his kitbag in one hand and a football in the other, and headed towards the changing room with Sammy. The room was a dilapidated Nissen hut that had an aroma of wintergreen ointment and perspiration. Dylan liked it, though, and felt it was somehow more real than the antiseptic changing room of his country club in America.

As he drew near the entrance he saw Gordon Elliott, a tall, tough, heavily built boy who was the centre forward on his team. Gordon had a slight smirk on his face and he indicated the departing Ford Granada.

'Did you give your chauffeur the night off?' he asked.

Dylan was aware that the other boy resented him. Because of his accent and clothes Gordon regarded him as a rich, spoiled American, but Dylan also suspected that it was to do with their different ways of playing soccer. Gordon was on old-style centre forward who relied on his bravery and brawn to bustle his way into goal-scoring opportunities. Dylan, however, was a winger who used his speed, trickiness and agility to out-manoeuvre opponents. 'Sissy football' he had heard Gordon describing it, which Dylan thought was really stupid. After all, the great George Best, the most famous player to come out of Belfast, was renowned for his skill and trickery, and he wasn't a sissy.

Dylan wasn't in the mood for arguing with Gordon, so he kept his tone light.

'No, tonight's my butler's night off. I never let the butler and the chauffeur off on the same night.'

Dylan was rewarded with a grin from Sammy, but Gordon wasn't amused.

'Think you're smart, don't you?'

'Would you prefer if I was stupid?'

'I'd prefer if you were normal,' said Gordon. 'Like the rest of us.'

'I am normal.'

'No you're not. You're a Jew.'

'And Jews aren't normal?'

'My da says they're bad news. And they had Jesus killed; it's in the bible.'

Dylan lowered his kitbag and breathed out, tying to think on his toes. He could normally count on Sammy's support, but Sammy could hardly be expected to come up with a defence of the Jewish race. He was going to have to get out of this one himself.

'What has killing Jesus got to do with me?' Dylan asked, keeping his tone reasonable.

'The Jews had him killed, and you're Jewish.'

'And Britt Ekland is Swedish,' said Dylan, naming the glamorous film star. 'Do you blame her because the Vikings killed Brian Boru?'

'Who's Brian Boru?'

'You're kidding me?' said Dylan, but he could see that Gordon really didn't know who he was talking about. 'Brian Boru was the High King of Ireland.'

'We don't care about Ireland up here. We're British.'

Dylan felt himself losing patience. 'Well, good for you. But it all happened ages ago. So I'm not to blame for Jesus, or Britt Ekland for the Vikings, or you for whatever your ancestors did! OK?'

Gordon didn't have a ready answer, and before he could think up something, Dylan dropped the football and kicked it on the volley against the wall of the Nissen hut. The bigger boy wasn't expecting the shot and he flinched slightly as the ball flew past him, then rebounded off the wall of the hut. Dylan took the ball on the rebound, skilfully tapped it twice on his foot, headed it up into the air, and then caught it in his hands. Sammy looked at him and winked in approval. Dylan resisted the temptation to smile, reckoning there was no point in making Gordon more of an enemy than necessary. Instead he gave Sammy a quick wink in return, hoisted up his kitbag and walked wordlessly past Gordon and into the changing room.

'Why was the Egyptian girl worried?'

Da tilted his head enquiringly, his eyes slightly glazed as he looked across the kitchen at Ma and Sammy. 'Well?'

Sammy tried to keep an amused look on his face. With his sisters gone to bed it was up to him and Ma to humour his father, as it often was when he drank too much.

'I don't know, Da,' Sammy answered, in a tone that suggested he was eager to hear the punch line.

'Why was the Egyptian girl worried?' repeated Da more insistently.

'Why was she worried, Bill?' said Ma.

'Because her daddy – was a mummy!'

Sammy and his mother laughed dutifully, and Da nodded, pleased with himself. 'Because her daddy was a mummy!' he repeated, as though the joke were somehow funnier for being said twice.

Sammy laughed again too, aware that his father's mood could swing very quickly, and knowing also that today was dole payment day, and that Da had spent too long in the pub.

'So, how was training?' his father asked. 'Buckie put you through your paces?'

Buckie was the nickname for Tom Buckley, the trainer in Sammy's soccer club, and a colourful ex-paratrooper that Da admired.

'Training was good,' answered Sammy, glad of the change of subject. 'Though Buckie nearly ran us into the ground.'

'Proper order', said Da. 'Hard training makes all the difference.'

Sammy thought this was a bit rich coming from Da, who hadn't kicked a ball in fifteen years. The back injury that stopped him from playing football had also cost Da his job in a foundry, so that now he sometimes got light casual work, but mostly he lived on unemployment payments.

'Hard training will make a man of you,' continued his father, in the voice he used when he felt he was dispensing words of wisdom.

'I know, Da. I'm not complaining. I'm just saying we could hardly walk by the time we finished. It was OK, though, I got a lift home.'

'Who gave you the lift?' queried Da.

'Dylan's father.'

Da snorted. 'Mr High-and-Mighty Goldman, swanning around in his fancy car. You don't need lifts from him.'

'He was only being obliging, Bill,' said Ma.

'Well I'd be obliged if he minded his own business. We're not depending on him.'

'I know, Da. But he was collecting Dylan, and Dylan is my friend, so he just—'

'Oh aye, Dylan is your friend!' interrupted Da. 'Or maybe he just became your friend so we could be guinea pigs for his aul" fella!'

'Bill,' said Ma softly but firmly, 'that's uncalled for.'

'Is it now?'

'Mr Goldman is a gentleman, and he's paid us well.'

'He doesn't bloody own us! Nobody buys off Bill Taylor!'

Sammy felt like shouting at his father, but he said nothing, knowing that this was a sore subject. Dylan's father was a newspaper journalist who also made radio programmes for the BBC and some of the American radio networks. As part of a series he was making on the emerging civil rights movement in Northern Ireland he was paying a fee – he called it a retainer – to have access to families in different parts of the city, so he could find out what life was like for ordinary people in Belfast. Despite working long hours at the mill, Sammy's mother wasn't well paid, and when Mr Goldman had politely made his proposal, Ma had insisted that Da go along with it.

It was an awkward arrangement, although if Mr Goldman thought that Da was just barely civil whenever he called, he didn't show it. And of course Ma tried to make up for Da's attitude, and willingly gave the journalist insights into how the people of their loyalist area felt.

'You know it's not like that, Bill,' said Ma now. 'Dylan is a very nice boy.'

'Oh yeah. "Hi there, Mr Taylor, how are you today?"' said Da, viciously mimicking Dylan's American accent. 'Gobdaw!'

'He's my friend,' said Sammy challengingly, stung by his father's cruelty.

'Don't you dare pull me up, sonny boy! Don't you dare!'

Sammy felt a bit intimidated but he wasn't going to back down completely.

'I'm just saying he's my friend.'

'And I'm saying I'm your da. I'm the boss here; I won't be cheeked in my own home.'

Ma raised her hand appeasingly. 'The child wasn't cheeking you, Bill. You've always taught him loyalty. Well, he was doing what you taught him, defending a friend.'

His father said nothing, and Sammy watched him, hoping he wouldn't get even more angry. Instead, Ma's words seemed to have worked, and his mood swung again.

'Sure, you're not the worst, Sammy,' he said, suddenly reaching out and tossing Sammy's hair affectionately. 'You're not the worst.'

Sammy forced a smile, relieved that Da's mood hadn't darkened further, but saddened that his father behaved like this. He suspected that it was to do with not having a job, and even though it was wrong to make comparisons, he couldn't help but wish that Da was more like Dylan's father. As soon as he thought it he felt guilty, then Da reached into his pocket and took out a bar of chocolate. He broke off a piece and handed it to Sammy.

'Here now, get that into you,' he said. 'Go on.'

'Thanks, Da,' answered Sammy, confused yet again by his unpredictable father, then he slipped the square into his mouth, turned away, and tried to concentrate on the sweet taste of the melting chocolate.

CHAPTER TWO

Maeve felt a thrill of excitement as she sized up the opposition. Some runners felt nervous before a race, but she loved the sense of competition and relished the moments leading up to the firing of the starting gun.

Today she was running at her home club of Ardara Harriers, whose track was a circuit around the sports field of a school off the Falls Road. Mr Doyle, the club trainer, took events like this so seriously that it might have been the Olympic Stadium. Maeve watched him now, bustling about the side of the track. He was a small, stocky man who ran a cobbler's shop and had six children, to whom he spoke Irish in a strong Belfast accent. He had thinning, curly hair that he combed over his balding head, and many people found it hard to believe that in his day he had been a noted runner who had almost made it into the Irish team for the 1948 Olympics.

'All set, Maeve?' he asked.

'Raring to go, Mr D.'

'*Maith an cailín*,' he said. 'And mind what I told you about being boxed in, all right?'

'I'll remember.'

The March afternoon sunshine was hazy and lacking in heat,

but Maeve was warmed up and ready to run. She had done all the pre-race exercises that Mr Doyle prescribed, and her muscles felt warm and nicely stretched. She watched now as the other runners – all girls of eleven or twelve years of age – made their final preparations, and she thought about the tactics she had agreed with Mr D. Don't make your move too soon, and don't get pushed around by Lucy Coyle.

Lucy Coyle was a fast runner who had a reputation for being rough and unsporting towards her opponents. Maeve didn't like her and had avoided her in the build up to the race. Coming towards the start of a race Maeve didn't like chatting too much, but she knew most of her opponents and usually exchanged a few words or a friendly nod.

Today there was only one competitor that she had never seen before, and Maeve watched the other girl now as she peeled off an expensive looking tracksuit. The girl was tall and slim, with pretty features and braces on her teeth. Something about her seemed different to the others, and Maeve made a mental note to be on guard against her, in case she was a top class runner from some distant club.

'Take your places, please!' cried the race organiser.

Mr Doyle approached Maeve and spoke in a quiet tone, asking the question he posed to all his runners before each competition. 'What are you here for, Maeve?'

'I'm here to win!'

'No better girl. Go and do it!'

Maeve nodded, then made her way briskly to the starting blocks, eager to be off and running.

Emma was shocked when the girl beside her elbowed her in the ribs. Back in America she had run in races where there had been jostling for position, but this was much more aggressive. Was this normal in Ireland? Emma hoped not, though she had no way of telling, as it was her first race since arriving in Belfast with her parents and her twin brother. She thought about retaliating, but the girl who had elbowed her had accelerated into the lead position and was now a couple of feet in front of everyone else.

Going into the last lap of the one mile race, Emma had felt confident. She could still win, she decided, as the blow to her ribs hadn't broken her stride. The rough girl who had hit her was heavily built and fast, but Emma was a strong finisher. There was still most of the last lap to go, and the best way to get revenge on the other girl would be to beat her.

Emma was in second place, running just ahead of a curly-haired girl in an Ardara Harriers singlet. Time to make a move. Emma put on a surge, closing the gap on the leader. She was conscious of the curly-haired girl speeding up to stay with her. She closed the gap on the girl who had elbowed her, then moved outside to overtake. This time she was ready to strike back if the girl tried to elbow her again. The other runners had speeded up in response, but Emma's pace was taking her into the lead. She kept her elbows in tight to her ribs, half expecting a jab that never came. Instead, just as she began to move to the front, she felt a kick to her ankle. Losing her balance, she tripped awkwardly. She tried desperately to stay upright, but her speed sent her sprawling, and she fell heavily onto the grass track.

Emma felt winded by the fall, then she took a blow to her back as another runner tripped over her and fell to the ground.

'No!' cried the other girl.

Emma looked up and saw that all of the other runners had managed to stay on their feet and had now streamed past. She felt angry that the lead runner had assaulted her again, but there was no chance of catching her now, no point even continuing the race.

'Are you OK?' said a voice.

Emma saw that the curly-haired girl who had been running at her shoulder was the person who had tripped over her.

'I think so,' she said, gingerly sitting up.

'That Lucy Coyle, I hate her!' said the other girl.

'Is she the one who tripped me?'

'Yeah, she's a right wee cow!'

'She sure is,' said Emma.

The curly-haired girl had dusted herself off and risen, and now she held out her hand to help Emma up.

'Thanks,' said Emma, rising to her feet a little shakily.

'Well, we're out of this race aren't we?' said the other girl with a wry grin.

'Yeah,' said Emma, 'and I could have won it.'

'You could have come second, you mean! I had the race sown up!'

Despite her frustration at being tripped, Emma found herself responding to the other girl's good humour, and she smiled back. 'We'll have to decide that another time.'

'OK, that's a deal. My name's Maeve.'

Emma immediately extended her hand. 'Emma Goldman,' she said, shaking hands as they began to walk back towards the far side of the track, where the spectators were gathered.

'Are you American?' asked Maeve.

'We lived in America, but my brother and I were born in England.'

'You sound dead American, it's brilliant.'

Emma grinned. 'Thanks. We were there for four years, so we picked up the accent.'

'I'm the same.'

'How do you mean?

'I've picked up the Belfast accent though I was born in Dublin.'

'How long are you here?'

'Three years. I've lived with my aunt and uncle since my mam died.'

'Oh, I'm sorry.'

'It's OK.'

Emma didn't want to pry, but her curiosity got the better of her. 'And what about your father?'

'Da's in the Irish army. He goes overseas with the United Nations, so I live with his sister, Aunt Nan, and Da comes up to

Belfast as much as he can.'

'Cool,' said Emma, impressed by the other girl's colourful background.

'So what brought you to Ireland?' asked Maeve.

'My dad writes for newspapers and makes radio programmes. He's here to cover the civil rights movement.'

'Gosh! I'd love a job like that.'

'Yeah, sometimes it's exciting. But a lot of it is politics, and really boring.'

'Right ...' agreed Maeve, though Emma could tell that the other girl still regarded her father's job as glamorous. Then Maeve looked her in the eye, suddenly changing the topic. 'So how come I haven't seen you at any other races?'

'This is my first one since getting here.'

'Yeah? What club are you with?'

'I haven't joined a club. I just heard about this race and decided to have a go.'

'You should join our club,' said Maeve. 'Ardara Harriers. I could introduce you to Mr D.'

'Who's Mr D?'

'He's our trainer. Some people think he's a bit of a header, but he knows his stuff.'

'What's a header?'

Maeve burst out laughing. 'A head case! But he's not really, he's just mad about running, and a bit, well ... a bit different. Do you want to meet him? It would be great if you joined.'

Emma was taken by the other girl's friendliness and enthusiasm, and she smiled. 'I'd love to meet a header! And I'd love to join too, but I'd have to ask my parents.'

'Are they here?'

'That's them over at the fence, looking worried,' said Emma as she and Maeve rounded the corner of the field.

'Why don't we say there's nothing to worry about, and ask can you join?'

'All right. But don't come straight out with it. They might have to be persuaded.'

'OK. Let's persuade them so.'

Emma smiled at Maeve, then made for her parents. Mom always said that every cloud had a silver lining, and today it seemed to be true. Emma was still disappointed about the race, but the silver lining was Maeve, and Emma had a feeling that she had just met a lively new friend.

'Don't be disgusting, Dylan,' said Mom, but she said it with a grin. Emma had to smile too as her twin brother pretended to be a cat, and licked clean the glass in which he had been served his ice-cream sundae.

They were all in Forte's Ice Cream Parlour as an after-race treat from Dad, to make up for Emma's disappointment at being tripped. Dad was also indulging his own sweet tooth, of course –

he particularly liked ice-cream – but Emma was grateful all the same. She had been really pleased when Dad had invited Maeve along, as a thank you for looking out for her when she fell, and Maeve had been glad to join them after reporting her version of what had happened to her trainer, Mr D, who was planning to lodge a complaint about Lucy Coyle.

Now Emma left aside her own ice-cream and spoke to her parents. 'Maeve runs with Ardara Harriers, she says it's a good club.'

'Really?' said Dad, then he turned to Maeve with genuine interest. 'And how long have you been running, Maeve?'

'About four years, Mr Goldman,' answered Maeve politely, and Emma could see that her parents were taken with the combination of Maeve's perky personality and her good manners.

'I didn't know anyone when I came to Belfast first,' continued Maeve, 'but it's a great way to make friends, and my Uncle Jim says it has me fit as a fiddle.'

'You've a lovely balanced stride all right,' said Mrs Goldman, 'we reckoned you were Emma's main rival in the race.'

'Got that one wrong, Mom', said Dylan chirpily, 'the Phantom Foot Tripper was the real rival!'

'You don't have to sound so pleased,' said Emma.

'Hey, if you hadn't been tripped we mightn't be eating ice-cream!'

Sometimes Emma found her twin really annoying, but she kept her impatience in check, concentrating instead on how to persuade her parents to let her join Maeve's club.

'I'd love to really get back into running,' she said, keeping her tone casual. 'Maybe I could join Ardara Harriers?'

Her father raised his eyebrows. 'Perhaps,' he said, then looked enquiringly at her mother.

'I'm sure it's a fine club, honey, but I don't know if you'd have the time. What with school, and tennis, and ballet.'

Emma had anticipated this and had her answer ready. 'But you only have to train once a week, Mom. You can do more if you want, but the junior club night is just once a week.'

Her mother nodded non-committedly, and Emma felt she had to do more.

'And it's not that far a drive from our house over to the Falls Road.' It was a very different part of the city, of course, with terraced two-up, two-down houses where Maeve lived, and detached suburban mansions in her own neighbourhood. But although Mom was from a rich New York family she wasn't snobbish, and Emma hoped that the location wouldn't be a problem.

'It's not the distance, Emma,' answered her mother, 'it's just I don't want you taking on too much.'

'You could always drop the ballet,' suggested Dylan.

'I like ballet.'

'It's pretty silly though, all that prancing on your toes.'

'I'm not asking you to do it!' Emma looked across the table to her father. 'And Dad, you said it was good for Dylan to meet Sammy and other boys from his neighbourhood in the soccer club. I just want to do the same.'

Dad shrugged. 'There is that,' he said, without actually agreeing to her proposal.

'What's your soccer club, Dylan?' asked Maeve.

'Wanderers. It's near Windsor Park.'

'Ah.'

'Do you know it?'

'I've heard of it,' answered Maeve, 'but that's a very loyalist area, so we don't go there much.'

Emma watched with interest as Maeve turned from Dylan to her parents. 'Maybe if Dylan is getting to meet boys from there, it would be good for Emma to meet people from my area?' she suggested reasonably.

Emma thought that this was a brilliant argument, and she felt like cheering Maeve for sensing that her parents wouldn't want to appear to discriminate against any group.

'Well, when you put it like that …' said Dad, and he looked to his wife.

'And I'd watch out for her, I promise,' added Maeve.

Mom laughed and raised her hands in surrender. 'OK, OK, I know when I'm beaten!'

'So I can join?'

'You can join.'

'Thanks, Mom!' said Emma, hugging her. 'Thanks, Dad.' She turned to Maeve who smiled and winked. Emma smiled back, then happily returned to her strawberry ice-cream, sure now that she and Maeve were going to be really good friends.

CHAPTER THREE

Sammy happily kicked a can as he walked along Ebor Street. His father had been given some temporary work, so the atmosphere at home today was happy. In a typical mood swing, Da had even promised to bring home sweets for Dylan and his sisters, Florrie, Ruby and Tess, after work this evening. Of course Da could easily forget, or his mood could change again, but Sammy had learned to live for the moment, and for now things felt good as he walked towards the football ground in the weak March sunshine.

Even though he wished that his father was more predictable – like Ma, whose affections he could always count on – part of him was fascinated by the idea of mood swings and how people's minds worked. He was aware that there were doctors who studied these things. He thought that it would be great to figure out why people behaved the way they did, and find ways to help them and make them happier. But although he would love a job like that, it was probably just a dream. Boys from his neighbourhood didn't become doctors. Instead they left school at fourteen or fifteen, with the lucky ones perhaps getting an apprenticeship, or a permanent job in one of the big factories or in Harland and Wolff's shipyard.

Sammy had never told anyone of his secret dream for fear of being ridiculed. Instead he protected himself by keeping his guard up, and appearing to everyone as the Sammy Taylor they thought they knew – tough, friendly, and a skilful but fearless full back for Wanderers football club. He crossed Tate's Avenue, lost in his thoughts, then he picked up his pace a little and approached the gates of the club, kitbag in hand.

'Mr Taylor. Good of you to join us!'

Sammy looked up to see Buckie, his trainer, looking at him with a hint of a grin.

Sammy knew that he wasn't late, but Buckie had been a sergeant in the paratroops and he had never lost the habit of keeping his charges on their toes. But he was fun too, and with his muscular build, drooping moustache and longish hair he cut a distinctive figure.

'Mr Buckley. Happy to join you,' Sammy said playfully.

'Cheeky wee bugger!' said the trainer, pointing at him.

Now that Buckie had raised his hand Sammy noticed that his right fist was bandaged. The other man saw Sammy staring, and he raised an eyebrow.

'Never seen bruised knuckles before?'

'Yes,' answered Sammy, then his curiosity got the better of him. 'Been in a scrap?'

'Nothing as lawless as a scrap,' answered Buckie. 'Out on duty with the Specials. Had to put manners on a couple of Taigs.'

Buckie was a part-time policeman with the B Specials, a force that Sammy knew was almost exclusively Protestant, and that had a reputation for its rough treatment of Taigs, the local word for Catholics.

'All these civil rights protests,' said Buckie. 'Just an excuse for the hooligans to take to the streets.'

'Right,' agreed Sammy, hoping the older man would give more detail.

'Well, last night we showed a couple of them who owns these streets!'

'Really?'

'Aye' said Buckie, and he was about to elaborate when he seemed to think better of it. 'Anyway, along with you and get changed.'

'OK,' answered Sammy, a little disappointed not to get more detail.

He carried on across the bumpy pitch and entered the draughty changing room where the rest of the boys were putting on their football gear. Gordon Elliot was lacing up a boot and he returned Sammy's greeting a little curtly. Sammy used to get on well with Gordon, but there had been a coolness in the centre forward's manner ever since Sammy had become friendly with Dylan. Sammy could never understand why being friendly with some-one new should affect those you were already friendly with – it wasn't like friendship was something that had to be rationed. But if Gordon disliked Dylan that was his problem, and Sammy wasn't going to be bullied by Gordon, or anyone else, in deciding who his friends were.

Moving down the dressing room now, he reached Dylan, who was pulling a football jersey over his head. Dylan grinned and pointed at Sammy. 'Hey, Sammy, I've a good one for you.'

'Yeah?'

'Hear about the mad scientist who kept dynamite in his fridge?'

'No.'

'He blew his cool!'

It was a really silly joke, but Sammy found himself laughing along with Dylan, and he suddenly realised how much he had come to like this colourful, English-born but American-sounding boy. He changed quickly into his own football gear, then a voice boomed out.

'All right, Ladies!'

The players looked up to see Buckie standing at the doorway, his hands on his hips.

'Let's be having you,' said the trainer, 'last one out does twenty press-ups!'

The boys stampeded for the door, and Sammy and Dylan laughingly jostled each other as they made for the pitch, each one determined not to be last.

'Aunt Nan, are you heartbroken?' Maeve said it with mock seriousness, and indicated the evening newspaper on the kitchen table. 'It says here that thousands of women are broken-hearted because Paul McCartney got married today.'

'Will you go way outta that,' said her aunt with a smile as she put away the crockery after their tea.

'Well, you told me Paul was your favourite Beatle,' said Maeve.

'He's nice and polite, I'll give him that.'

'Nothing to do with being the best-looking Beatle?' queried Maeve.

'Have you nothing better to do than torment me?' asked her aunt.

'I've training – but tormenting you is more fun!'

'No, you've got it all wrong, Maeve,' said Uncle Jim, who had been sitting in the armchair puffing on his sweet-smelling pipe. 'Forget your Paul McCartneys; Bing Crosby is the singer I had to compete with when I met your aunt.'

'Bing Crosby?' said Maeve. 'Sure he's ancient!'

'I beg your pardon!' retorted Aunt Nan, 'he's nothing of the sort.'

'What did I tell you?' said Uncle Jim, 'still has a soft spot for him!'

'You're both hilarious,' said Aunt Nan, then she indicated the newspaper. 'Who did he marry anyway?'

Maeve picked up the paper and read aloud. 'McCartney, 27, married Linda Eastman, eldest daughter of a wealthy American family.'

'Good man yourself!' said Uncle Jim.

'She's a professional photographer from New York,' continued Maeve, 'and it says the groom wore a grey suit and a yellow tie, and the bride wore a beige dress and a daffodil yellow coat.'

'A beige dress?' said Aunt Maeve. 'What ails her?'

Maeve considered for a second. 'She's probably a fashion leader.'

Uncle Jim nodded as though he were serious. 'In fairness, the yellow overcoat sounds good. Might get one of those myself!'

Maeve laughed, and Aunt Nan looked at her husband.

'You're a right-looking article without a yellow overcoat,' she said, but Maeve knew that Aunt Nan was amused.

She liked moments like these when the three of them were together, and when her hard working uncle and occasionally strict aunt were relaxed. She would have liked to linger, and maybe get Uncle Jim to reveal more about her aunt being taken with Bing Crosby when she was young, but she had arranged to meet her new friend Emma at the Ardara Harriers grounds. Reluctantly she put the newspaper aside and rose from the table.

'I better get my gear,' she said.

'I whitened your runners,' said Aunt Nan, 'they're beside your bed.'

'Thanks, that's great,' said Maeve. 'But I still think you're heart-broken!'

Before her aunt could reply Maeve laughed and ducked out of the room. She ran up the stairs, slipped the newly cleaned runners into her sports bag, and descended the stairs again. 'Bye!' she cried.

'Bye, Maeve,' answered her uncle from the kitchen.

'Don't forget to bless yourself!' called her aunt, and Maeve quickly crossed herself from the holy water font on the wall beside the front door, then exited onto Bombay Street.

She made her way past rows of terraced houses, smoke rising from the chimneys and hanging in the early evening air. The light outside was fading and the house interiors looked cosy as Maeve glanced in through front windows and saw coal fires and warmly lit rooms. She passed by the imposing edifice of Clonard Monastery, then reached the Falls Road and headed towards the sports ground.

She hoped that Emma would show up tonight as arranged, and that nothing had happened to make either Emma or her parents change their minds. After the ice creams in Forte's the previous week, Emma's mother had asked for Maeve's telephone number, in case any problem arose. Maeve had been slightly embarrassed to have to explain they didn't have a phone, though in emergencies they had access to one of their neighbours who did.

She had heard nothing however, and now Maeve turned in the gate to the Ardara Harriers grounds. There was no sign of Emma. Several of the other girls in the club were already there and Maeve exchanged greetings with them, then suddenly her heart lifted when she saw the slim form of Emma coming in through the entrance. She was wearing a stylish, light blue tracksuit, and Maeve saw the other girls looking at her curiously.

'She's a friend of mine who's joining,' she explained. 'Be nice to her, girls, OK?'

Before anyone could respond, Maeve saw Mr D intercepting Emma. She hurried to join them, wanting to be sure that the trainer wouldn't say anything to put Emma off before she even began.

'Hello, Emma,' she said, 'hello, Mister Doyle.'

'Hi,' said Emma with a warm smile.

Behind the braces her teeth were pearly white, Maeve noticed, then Mr D turned around.

'*Maith an cailín*, Maeve,' he said.

Maeve could see that Emma was bemused. 'It means "good girl",' she explained. 'Mr D likes to slip in a bit of Irish now and then.'

'Why wouldn't I? Isn't it our native tongue?' he said, looking at Maeve with the slightly bulging-eyed looked that helped to make him appear eccentric.

Maeve could have argued that for the vast majority of people in Ireland English was their native language, and that it was only in the scattered Gaeltacht regions that people were native Irish speakers. Instead she nodded in agreement. 'No reason why you wouldn't speak Irish, Mr D, I'm sure Emma loved hearing it.'

She looked at Emma and winked, and the other girl proved quick on the uptake.

'Yes, it sounds fascinating. Like, a really musical language.'

Maeve could see that Mr D was pleased and she smiled at the trainer. 'Emma has come from Washington to live in Ireland, so I asked her along tonight.'

'*Ceart go leor,*' said Mr D. 'You're welcome, Emma.'

'Thanks.'

'I saw you run in the race last week. Good acceleration, but you need to work on your technique.'

'Right,' said Emma.

'Maybe you could help her, Mister D, the way you've helped me,' suggested Maeve.

'Maybe I could,' answered Mr D. 'Then again maybe I couldn't. It all depends on you,' he said, turning his bulging gaze to the other girl. 'Are you prepared to really work on it? Do you want success?

'Sure I do.'

Maeve watched as the trainer stared appraisingly at Emma. Suddenly he nodded as though satisfied with what he saw.

'Fine then. Join Maeve, and we'll start training in five minutes.' Before Emma could respond, the trainer turned away and moved off briskly.

'Wow,' said Emma with a grin. 'He's eh … he's kind of different, isn't he?'

Maeve smiled back. 'I told you he can seem a bit mad. But he's a good trainer, he'll speed you up if you do what he says.'

'OK, count me in.'

'Brilliant.' Maeve put her arm around Emma's shoulder. 'Welcome to the Harriers!'

CHAPTER FOUR

'Aw come on, Dad!' said Dylan, 'not another recording!'

'You'll thank me when you're older,' answered his father laughingly as he came into the Goldmans' dining room and began filming Dylan, Emma and their mother with his cine camera.

The lunch was to celebrate St Patrick's Day, and Mom had set a delicious-looking apple pie on the table, but Dylan felt that his father overdid the family films.

'When I'm pushing up the daisies,' said Dad, 'you'll play these reels and—'

'No I won't!' interjected Dylan.

His father ignored the interruption and continued in a mock tragic voice. 'And you'll cry bitter tears that you weren't nicer to your saintly father while he lived!'

Dylan's mother laughed. 'Dad is right; it's good to record stuff. And hey, it's St Patrick's Day, and we're in Ireland, we have to mark the occasion.'

'Couldn't we mark it by going to a movie, or bowling or something?' suggested Emma.

'We can do those things any time, honey,' Mom answered.

Dylan watched as his mother now turned from Emma and struck a dramatic pose, while his father filmed.

'Ready for my close-up, Mr DeMille,' she proclaimed.

Although part of him thought it was corny to be filming these family occasions, Dylan still enjoyed his mother's sense of fun and Dad's wacky humour, even if he didn't admit it to his parents. And in many ways he was lucky. They lived in a large house on the Malone Road, there was no shortage of money, the lunch table was laden with food and sunshine flooded in from the landscaped back garden, filling the room with warm golden light. Deciding to be more positive, he smiled as his father panned the camera and Emma pulled a face.

'Lovely,' said Dad, 'glad I got that.' He switched off the cine camera and put it down on the table.

'Here, before we eat – a Patrick's Day joke,' said his mother. 'Why did St Patrick drive all the snakes out of Ireland?'

'Why?'

'He couldn't afford the plane fare!'

'Mom, that is so lame,' said Emma.

'Why did the leprechaun cross the road,' continued his mother unabashed.

'Why did the leprechaun cross the road?' repeated Dad, in the style of a comedian's assistant.

'He wanted to reach the crock of gold faster!'

'Mom, this is cruelty to children,' said Emma, but Dylan thought the joke was so daft that it was sort of funny.

Mom raised her glass. 'Here's to St Patrick. Like the song says, it's a great day for the Irish.'

'But that's the weird thing,' said Dylan. 'It's not that great a day here in Belfast. Not compared to New York last year.'

'Well … that's a little bit complicated,' said Dad.

'How do you mean?'

'In the States, people are happy to be Irish for the day,' explained his father. 'But in Belfast some people feel being Irish would make them seem less British. So they don't make a fuss about St Patrick's Day. They don't see it as part of their culture.'

'So why are we celebrating it?' asked Emma. 'It's not part of our culture either.'

'But we're living here,' said Mom. 'And it's part of Ireland's culture. And Northern Ireland is still in Ireland.'

'OK,' said Emma. 'But it makes you think. Like, where are we from? What's our home?

This was something Dylan wondered about too and he looked to his father who replied thoughtfully.

'When you get down to it, home is really where your family is.'

'That's OK for you, Dad,' said Dylan. 'Your family is in Leeds where you grew up. Just like Mom grew up with her family in New York.'

'But we're always moving,' chipped in Emma. 'So where are Dylan and me supposed to be from?'

'Well, you were born in England, so you're British citizens,' answered their father.

'But we don't sound English, Dad,' said Dylan, ''cause we've lived in different parts of the States. We're always moving.'

His father shrugged. 'That's my job, Dylan. I go to where history is being made.'

'And you're getting a chance to see interesting places, different peoples,' said Mom.

Dylan was tempted to say that he had seen enough interesting places, but he remembered his earlier thoughts about how lucky he was and decided not to ruin Mom's Patrick's Day celebration.

'Try not to see moving as a problem, more an opportunity,' said his father.

'Right,' answered Dylan. He half expected Emma to keep up the argument, but she had been in good form ever since making friends with Maeve Kennedy and joining the running club, and now she let the matter drop.

'Tell you what,' said Mom. 'How about we have a treat?'

'Yeah?' said Dylan.

'For the day that's in it,' she said with a straight face, 'what about a double helping of bacon and cabbage for dinner?!'

'And all the buttermilk you can drink!' said Dad in a phoney Irish accent.

Dylan smiled but Emma tried to sound annoyed.

'That's not funny,' she said.

'With fried shamrock, and lightly grilled leprechaun!' added Dad.

This time Dylan laughed and his sister couldn't help but join in.

'And maybe after lunch we'll take in a movie and have a Wimpy on the way home?' suggested Mom.

Dylan felt a surge of affection for her and gave her a thumbs up sign. 'Now you're talking!'

'But first you have to say it,' said Dad.

'Say what?'

'Top of the mornin'!'

'That's so stage Irish, Dad,' said Emma.

'I know, but there you are. So – a movie, a wimpy, and I'll even throw in a box of Maltesers. What do you say?'

Dylan didn't hesitate. 'Bejapers and begorrah, the top of the mornin' to you!'

'Done,' said his father. 'Happy St Patrick's Day!'

Sammy knew he was in trouble. Every Saturday afternoon he worked as a messenger boy for Smyth's grocery store in the city centre, and today he had taken a risk on his way back from a delivery. Most of Smyth's customers lived in loyalist areas, but Sammy had cut through a nationalist neighbourhood, his interest aroused by the sight of young men holding aloft the kind of placards he had seen on protest marches on television. He had cycled in their direction, but before he knew what was happening five boys of about his own age had surrounded his bike, and he had immediately cursed himself for his curiosity.

There had been a protest march earlier, during which the police had clashed again with nationalists demanding civil rights. In spite of his loyalist upbringing, part of Sammy couldn't help but feel sympathy for them. The marchers demand for one-man-one-vote didn't seem that much to ask, even though Da said that if they got that, then thousands of Catholics would push for better housing and jobs, and it would be working-class Protestants like themselves who would lose out. Sammy hadn't argued back, not wanting to annoy his father. But though he understood Da's concern, he thought one-man-one-vote was only fair, and that maybe the police shouldn't be so willing to baton civil rights marchers.

He had entertained those thoughts at lunch time, in the safety of his own home, but now his sympathy was replaced by fear, as the nationalist boys moved in on him.

'What have we got here?' said their leader, a tall boy with red hair and a strutting walk.

'What are you doing on our street?' said his sidekick, a smaller, stocky boy with a turn in his eye.

The three other boys had positioned themselves to the side and behind him, but a quick look told Sammy that the first two boys were the ones that mattered. Despite the fact that his heart was racing, Sammy smiled and tried to sound casual.

'Maybe you can help me, lads,' he said. 'I'm heading for Castle Street, but I took a wrong turn.'

'Yeah, I think maybe you did,' said the red-haired boy with a smirk.

'Smyth's grocers,' said his stocky friend, reading the name from the advertising sign on Sammy's bicycle. 'I've never seen you delivering here before.'

'No,' answered Sammy, trying to keep his tone relaxed, 'I normally don't do this area. 'What's the quickest way back into town?'

'Don't be in such a hurry,' said Red Head, placing his hand on the handlebars.

'I'm not in a hurry, just asking for directions.'

'We'll give directions when we're ready. Where do you normally deliver?'

Sammy hesitated, not wanting to reveal that it was exclusively loyalist areas that he serviced for Smyth's. 'Wherever I'm sent,' he answered with a shrug. 'All over the city, really.'

'Wherever you're sent? That sounds like a smart answer, pal,' said Red Head, and Sammy could see the other boys smiling, aware that their leader was trying to pick a fight.

'I'm not trying to be smart. I'm just doing a job, lads,' said Sammy.

'You're doing a job for Smyth's,' answered the stocky boy. 'That sounds like a Protestant name. Are you a Prod too?'

Sammy shook his head. If he admitted his religion this would end badly. 'Smyth's are a Protestant firm,' he replied, 'but they hire Catholics as messenger boys.'

'So you're a Catholic then?' said Red Head.

'Yeah.'

'Where do you live?'

'Short Strand,' answered Sammy, opting for the most distant nationalist area he could think of.

'So you wouldn't have much time for the Queen?'

'No.'

'Say "To hell with the Queen" then.'

Sammy hated doing it, but he had no choice, and so he answered. 'To hell with the Queen.'

Red Head looked him in the eye, and Sammy wasn't sure if he had convinced the other boy. Red Head held his gaze, then reached into his pocket and took out a coin. He turned it over so that the image of the queen was uppermost, then held it out towards Sammy. 'Spit on the Queen,' he said.

Sammy hesitated, something inside him rebelling.

'I knew it,' said the other boy triumphantly. 'You're a little Prod.'

'Know what we do with Prods?' asked the stocky boy, but Sammy didn't respond. Although he could feel his mouth going dry and his heart thumping, he was trying to think clearly. He remembered something that his trainer, Buckie, had told him when reminiscing about his days as a paratrooper. *Take the initiative when the enemy least expects it.* If he was to get out of this he had to find the courage to take the initiative.

'Look, you've got this all wrong, lads,' Sammy said, dismounting from the bicycle and propping it up. 'The reason I didn't want to spit, is that–'

But Sammy never finished the sentence. Lunging forward with all his strength, he punched Red Head in the stomach and saw the bigger boy doubling up with a gasp of pain. Spinning around, Sammy gave a full force kick in the shins to the stocky boy, who screamed out in agony, then dropped to one knee, holding his leg. Sammy had counted on the other three boys being followers rather than leaders, and sure enough, with the two toughest members out of action, they hesitated as Sammy grabbed the bicycle and pulled it off the stand. He drove it straight at the nearest boy who jumped out of the way, then Sammy mounted the bicycle and pedalled furiously down the road. He glanced over his shoulder and saw Red Head still doubled up, and the stocky boy clutching his shin. 'God Save the Queen!' cried Sammy, then he cycled as fast as he could towards the main road and safety.

CHAPTER FIVE

'Emma, turn down the volume!'

'Ah, Dad.'

'It's background music, not an outside broadcast!'

Emma looked appealingly at her father. 'It's the Beach Boys, Dad, they go with barbecues.'

'Never argue with a man carrying barbecue tongs!' said her father, advancing across the lawn in mock threat. 'Now lower it and don't sneak up the volume again!'

'All right, all right!' Emma said making for the door of the kitchen.

The spring sunshine bathed the back garden with warmth, and although she pretended to be annoyed, Emma was actually in good form. She had loved barbecues when they lived in America, and this was the first one her parents had held since coming to Belfast. Lots of the adults had arrived already, with some chatting in the garden, some clustered around her father as he tended the delicious-smelling steaks on the barbecue, while others greeted her mother who was dispensing drinks from the kitchen.

Dylan and his friend Sammy were organising golf balls and a target for a putting competition, and Emma said, 'Don't forget the left handed club for me,' as she passed them.

'It's all the one, you haven't a hope of winning!' said her twin brother, but Emma ignored him as she went to the stereo system and lowered the volume. It was The Beach Boys latest hit, 'Do it Again', and Emma thought it was a brilliant song. Why did old people like Dad never want to hear good music played loudly? Would there come a day when she would be like that? She hoped never to be that old-fashioned, then her thoughts were disturbed when she heard the doorbell ringing.

'I'll get it!' she cried, moving excitedly down the hall towards the front door. She had enjoyed the company of her new friend Maeve Kennedy over the last couple of weeks, and had invited her to the Sunday barbecue. She liked Maeve's enthusiasm and how the other girl managed to find some fun even in the tough training drills they did in the running club. She opened the heavy oak hall door now, and there was her friend, her freckled face wreathed in a smile and her curly brown hair tied up with two yellow ribbons.

'Hi, Maeve,' she said.

'Emma – your house is huge!'

Emma took her home for granted, but now, seeing it through Maeve's eyes, she realised how her family must appear rich compared to Maeve's. What did that matter though if you were friends? 'Come on in,' she said, 'and I'll show you around.'

'Thanks', said Maeve,' stepping into the hallway. 'But first I've to give this to your ma.'

'What is it?'

'Two jars of homemade marmalade from my Aunt Nan.'

'OK.'

Emma led the way down the hall, then brought Maeve to where her mother was stirring fruit in a bowl of punch. 'Mom, Maeve has something for you.'

'Hello, Mrs Goldman. Just a little present from my aunt,' said Maeve, handing over the wrapped jars.

'Thank you, honey. There was no need, but thank your aunt very much all the same.'

'I will.'

'Come on and I'll get you a drink,' said Emma. 'If you stay here any longer Mom will start telling you Patrick's Day jokes.'

Maeve grinned at Emma. 'Well, I loved the one you told me about the sleepy leprechaun.'

'Hey, this is a girl after my own heart!' cried Mom. 'Give her a double helping!'

Despite Mom's corny jokes, Emma liked the way her mother was always welcoming, and now she happily led Maeve to the far side of the kitchen, where rows of soft drinks were laid out on a table. 'Coke, Pepsi, orange, lemonade? What will you have?'

'Eh … orange please.'

Emma poured her friend a glass of a fizzy local orange drink, then popped in some ice cubes. 'Fancy a sly cupcake before the barbecue?'

'If I knew what a cupcake was.'

Emma was amazed. 'Never heard of a cupcake?'

Maeve made an earnest face. 'Cross my heart and hope to die in a barrel of rats!'

Emma laughed. 'It's a little sponge cake with icing. Look,' she said, leading Maeve to a corner of the kitchen and lifting the lid on a large tray of ornately iced cakes.

'Oh, they're like fairy cakes, only fancier.'

'We'll scoff one each before anyone sees us,' Emma said, handing one to Maeve and eating one herself.

'Mmm,' said Maeve, 'absolutely gorgeous!'

'Yeah. And you've never heard them called cupcakes?'

'No. But then I've never been to a barbecue either.'

'We had them all the time in America. Wait till you taste Dad's barbecued steaks.'

'Can't wait.'

'And Dylan and his friend Sammy are setting up a putting competition. Will we take them on?'

'Are they any good?'

'They're boys, so they think they're great at everything.'

'OK', said Maeve. 'Let's teach them a lesson!'

'You're on!' said Emma, glad already that she had invited her new friend to the barbecue.

The thump of an explosion sounded in the distance, and Emma quickly turned to her brother. 'Was that … was that a bomb?'

'I'd say so,' answered Dylan.

In spite of herself Emma felt a little bit excited at something so dramatic, but she knew that this was a bad development. And though the sound came from far away, she sensed a ripple of unease running through the guests at the barbecue.

It was a pity, because everything had gone really well. The food had been delicious, and she and Maeve had beaten Dylan and Sammy by two points in a competitive and highly enjoyable putting competition. It had only been when she had introduced them that it occurred to her that Maeve was from a nationalist area and Sammy from a loyalist one. Ever since coming to Belfast, however, Emma had felt that most of the trouble between Catholics and Protestants made no sense, and she had been pleased when Maeve and Sammy had gotten on well.

'They've probably attacked another water reservoir,' said Sammy.

'What a daft thing to attack,' said Dylan, and for once Emma had to agree with her brother.

Tension had been rising because of the civil rights protests, and over the previous few weeks there had been several bomb attacks on reservoirs, causing water shortages in Belfast and parts of county Down.

'Daft is right, but that's the IRA for you,' said Sammy.

Emma had heard her father talking about the IRA and knew that it stood for the Irish Republican Army, an armed group that wanted the British to leave Northern Ireland.

'Who says it was the IRA?' asked Maeve.

'My da told me,' answered Sammy.

'My uncle heard it could be the UVF,' argued Maeve.

Emma looked at Maeve in surprise. The UVF was a loyalist armed group, and loyalists were in favour of Northern Ireland keeping the link with Britain.

'But why would the UVF bomb reservoirs? They're not against the government?'

'They're doing it so the IRA will get the blame. That's what Uncle Jim heard.'

'That's crazy,' said Sammy.

'Why is it crazy?' queried Maeve

'It just is.'

'That's not much of an argument, Sammy.'

Emma wished there didn't have to be any argument at all, but before she could intervene Sammy spoke again. 'It's just lies they made up.'

'My uncle doesn't tell lies.'

'I'm not saying he does,' said Sammy. 'But what he was told is a lie. The IRA just want to shift the blame.'

'IRA, UVF – why can't they butt out?' asked Dylan. 'Let the government and the civil rights people do a deal, and leave us all in peace?'

'Exactly,' said Emma, pleased that her brother had put into words what she thought, and hoping that this disagreement wouldn't break up their foursome. Although she and Dylan had met other children in school and at the local tennis club, in both places factions were already formed. She and Dylan were the new kids – not quite excluded – but not really part of the 'in gang'. Now, with

Sammy and Maeve, Emma had hoped to have her own little gang, and she didn't want to see things spoiled.

'Let's not fight over any of this stuff, it's too stupid,' she said. 'Can we all just be friends?'

She looked at Maeve. There was a brief pause, then to her relief Maeve smiled and said 'OK.'

'Sammy?'

The other boy looked at her, and she feared he was going to argue. Then he shrugged his shoulders and gave a wry smile. 'Yeah, why not?' he said.

'Great,' answered Emma. 'And just to celebrate it, let's have another game of putting. Think you could beat us girls this time?'

'You only won by a fluke the last time,' said Dylan.

'OK, Maeve, let's show them, yeah?'

'Absolutely.'

'Right, boys' said Emma, 'get ready for a beating!'

CHAPTER SIX

'I don't like Good Friday,' said Maeve, 'it always feels kind of gloomy.'

'Really, Maeve,' said Aunt Nan reprovingly. 'It's the day Our Lord died for our sins; of course it's a sad day.'

They were sitting at the kitchen table having a dinner of fried fish – meat being forbidden on Good Friday – and Uncle Jim pushed his empty plate aside and looked at Maeve.

'Sure Lent is a doddle nowadays. Years ago we didn't just fast on Ash Wednesday and Good Friday, we fasted all forty days of Lent.'

'And we went without meat,' added Aunt Nan proudly. 'Fasting and abstaining, it was called.'

Maeve thought this sounded a bit extreme. She didn't mind skipping meat for a day. In fact, she had gorged so much on steak the previous Sunday at Emma's barbecue that it only felt like balancing things out. But forty days of fasting and abstaining?

'I'm not being cheeky, Aunt Nan,' she said, 'but why all that fasting?'

'To atone for our sins.'

'But we don't do it any more.'

'No, they changed the rule,' said Uncle Jim. 'Thanks be to God!'

'Jim,' said Aunt Nan reproachfully.

Maeve's aunt was more religious than her uncle, and so Maeve posed her question to her now. 'I'm glad they changed the rule,' she said. 'But why did they? Have people not as many sins to atone for now?'

Aunt Nan looked slightly taken aback. 'I'm sure people today have as many sins – probably more. But the Church decided that God is so merciful we only need to fast and abstain for two days during Lent. Though, of course, you should make other sacrifices instead.'

'Right.'

'What brought all this on?' asked Uncle Jim.

'I was just thinking about different religions,' said Maeve. 'Emma's mother decided to be a Buddhist, so she doesn't have to worry about any of this.'

'Well, we'll see where that gets her on the Last Day,' said Aunt Nan.

'Mrs Goldman's a really nice woman. I'm sure she'll get into heaven,' answered Maeve.

'I'm not even certain what Buddhists believe in,' mused Uncle Jim. 'Well, apart from believing in Buddha.'

'Emma said it's about being at one with the universe, and Karma, and all that.'

'Who's Karma when he's at home?' asked her uncle.

'It's not a person, Uncle Jim. I think it's like … like fate, or luck.'

'I hope they're not filling your head with notions,' said Aunt Nan. 'Your dad trusted me to bring you up as a good Catholic, and if these people are leading you astray...'

'It's not like that at all,' said Maeve quickly. Her aunt and uncle approved of her friendship with Emma, and had been impressed by the fact that Mr Goldman wrote newspaper articles and did broadcasts on the radio. But that agreement could change very rapidly if Aunt Nan thought Maeve's faith was at risk. She needed to put her mind at rest at once. 'Mrs Goldman never even mentioned Buddha to me. Emma doesn't think she's that serious about it really.'

Aunt Nan frowned. 'Well, not being serious about her religion is hardly to her credit.'

'Yeah, if you're going to be a Buddhist you might as well be a proper one,' said Uncle Jim.

This whole conversation was heading in the wrong direction, Maeve thought with alarm. She loved being friends with Emma Goldman. She had really enjoyed the barbecue and the family's glamorous American ways, and it had been great fun competing in the putting competition with Dylan and his friend Sammy, despite the disagreement about the IRA and the UVF. Maeve couldn't risk not being allowed to stay friends with Emma. Time to distract her aunt and uncle. 'No one talked about religion at the barbecue,' she reassured them. 'But Mr Goldman said something that was really interesting.'

'What was that?' Uncle Jim asked.

'He's doing articles for the *Guardian* newspaper, about next week's election. And he thinks Bernadette Devlin will get elected.'

'Really?' said Aunt Nan.

Bernadette Devlin was a twenty-one year old nationalist, and a passionate campaigner for civil rights. If successful in the Westminster elections she would be the youngest Member of Parliament in history.

'That would be one in the eye for the other crowd,' said Uncle Jim with gusto.

'Wouldn't it just?' said Aunt Nan.

Her aunt and uncle began discussing Bernadette Devlin, and Maeve breathed a quiet sigh of relief, hopeful now that she had distracted them – and eased the threat to her friendship with Emma.

'You're just a stupid show-off!' said Gordon as the team trooped into the changing hut after training.

Dylan was stung and he turned to face the other boy. 'What's it to you?'

Gordon drew nearer, his manner threatening. 'What's it to me?'

'Yeah,' answered Dylan, unwilling to back down.

'This is my club. You don't belong here; you're just a blow-in Yank!'

'You can't even get that much right,' said Dylan.

'What?'

'I'm not a Yank, I was born in England.'

'I don't care where you were born! You don't fit in here. And if you pull a stunt like that in a real match I'll break your face!'

Dylan had done a fancy move to wrong-foot the goalkeeper during the seven–a-side game that ended training. Emma and Maeve had come in the car with his mother to collect him, and maybe their presence had caused him to show off a little. But he had scored a stylish goal, and Buckie hadn't complained, so he wasn't going to apologise to Gordon. Besides, taking exception to the fancy move was only an excuse. Gordon just didn't like him, and if it wasn't this, it would be something else that he would use to start an argument.

'Take it easy, lads,' said Sammy, 'Buckie will hear you.'

'He won't,' said Vic Balfe. 'He's putting away the nets.'

Vic was the goalkeeper that Dylan had wrong-footed, and also one of Gordon's friends, and it was obvious that he wanted trouble. Dylan realised that Sammy had been trying to use Buckie to defuse the situation. Now, though, there was no way to back down from Gordon's threat without losing face.

'I'll play soccer any way I please,' said Dylan, forcing himself to sound unworried. 'And you can like it or lump it.'

Gordon suddenly pushed him in the shoulder. 'Maybe I'll lump it then!'

Dylan managed to keep his balance, but before he could react Sammy spoke again.

'Come on, lads, this is stupid.'

'Stay out of it, Sammy, this is between me and him,' said Gordon. Sammy looked to Dylan, and even though Gordon was intimidating, Dylan felt that he couldn't let his friend fight his battles for him.

'It's OK, Sammy,' he said quietly. 'I'll handle this.'

'Will you now? Let's see you try.'

'Have a scrap here and Buckie could suspend the whole team! We're not having that,' said Sammy.

Buckie was really strict about discipline, and Dylan thought that this was a clever argument by Sammy to prevent a fight.

'Fine,' said Gordon. 'We'll do it in the gym.' He drew closer to Dylan and pointed his finger aggressively. 'Three rounds in the ring, Yank. Unless you're chicken? Well?'

'Fine,' snapped Dylan. 'Three rounds it is!'

CHAPTER SEVEN

'Move the rabbit's ears, Sammy, you're the expert!'

Sammy fiddled with the small aerial that stood on top of the family's television, its two slanting prongs earning it the nickname 'rabbit's ears', and the distortion on the screen lessened. He shifted the aerial a little more, then suddenly the black and white image on the television screen became much clearer.

'Da-dah!' said Sammy playfully, and Ma laughed.

He liked Friday nights. Da always went to the pub, and when Sammy's sisters were in bed he was allowed to stay up watching television with his mother. Ma's favourite programme was 'The Saint', starring Roger Moore, and Sammy's favourite was 'Thunderbirds', but on Friday nights they watched any light entertainment that was on, and Sammy enjoyed it when they relaxed together.

Now the fire was burning cosily, and they were tuned into a variety show, with Louis Armstrong singing his hit from the previous year, 'What a Wonderful World'.

'I love that song,' said Ma.

'Me too', agreed Sammy. He didn't normally like the old fashioned jazz that Louis Armstrong did, but 'What a Wonderful World' somehow seemed to suit his rasping style, and the song had been massively successful.

His mother rarely sang aloud, though if really pressed, her party piece was 'Softly, Softly', which had been a number one hit for a local Belfast woman, Ruby Murray. Sammy watched now as she happily hummed along with Louis Armstrong, then she looked at him and grinned.

'I know I'm a bit of a frog,' she said, 'but it's a lovely tune. Pity people don't heed the words,' she added ruefully.

'Yeah,' said Sammy, 'it is.'

Even though it was just a pop song, 'What a Wonderful World' was a kind of plea for tolerance. Sammy wished there was a bit more of that going around. He thought of the incident with Dylan and Gordon and wondered, yet again, if there was some way he could save his friend. Gordon was an accomplished boxer, and Sammy feared that Dylan would end up getting hurt if he went ahead with the boxing match. But Dylan had accepted the challenge, and his friend would have no standing in the soccer club if he backed out now.

Sammy wondered why Gordon disliked Dylan so much. Certainly Dylan was different to the other boys on the team. Why should it be a problem, though, that someone came from a different group to your own? But Sammy knew it was a problem, whether in Wanderers soccer club or in Belfast in general. And he was honest enough to recognise that he wasn't immune to it himself – he had enjoyed taunting the nationalist boys after his escape from them on his bike.

It was all the more reason, he thought now, why he would love to study medicine and find out how people's minds worked. But though that was just a dream, lately he had been thinking about it more frequently.

'You're a million miles away, Sammy,' said Ma with a smile.

'Sorry.'

'What's running through that head of yours?'

'Just … just thinking about the football club.' It was only a white lie, but he wasn't sure if Ma fully believed him.

She looked at him sympathetically. 'You'd tell me if there was something you needed to talk about?'

'Yeah.' Sammy hesitated. Part of him wanted to tell his mother of his dream of being a doctor. But while she wouldn't make fun of him, she might think he was getting notions about himself. Or maybe she would want to back him to the hilt, and would try to raise money they couldn't afford for books and college expenses. He wasn't sure what to do. It would be good to share his dream with someone, and this was a perfect opportunity. He hesitated, but before he could make a decision he heard the sound of the hall door opening.

'There you are!' said his father, his speech slightly slurred by drink as he entered the cosy front room.

Sammy knew at once that the moment for confiding in his mother was gone. In one way he was disappointed, in another relieved. Before he could think about it any further his father flopped down into the armchair.

'What's this rubbish?' he asked, indicating the television.

'Just a variety show,' said Ma. 'I'll turn it off.'

Sammy hated the way Ma gave way to him like that, although he understood that it made sense not to cross Da after he had been drinking. His father wasn't quite drunk now, but his eyes had the glazed look that told Sammy he had had a fair bit to drink.

'What's the news, Da?' he said, aware that his father liked to be thought of as someone with the latest word on what was happening in Belfast.

'Same as every night lately. Bloody Taigs losing the run of themselves!'

'Bill,' said Ma in mild reproach.

'Well, they are. Marching and demanding their rights? Who do they think they are?' Sammy said nothing, but he thought of Emma's friend Maeve. He had never told his parents about socialising with a Catholic girl, and even though he had argued a little with Maeve about who planted the bombs at the water reservoirs, he had liked her lively personality.

'We're going to have to put the Taigs in their place,' continued Da. 'And there're plenty of lads willing to do it.'

'Please, Bill,' said Ma. 'Don't get mixed up in trouble.'

'We're not the ones causing the trouble!' said Da argumentatively. 'But there'll be blood on the streets; it's only a matter of time.' Suddenly Da's mind shifted and he looked enquiringly at Ma. 'Have you anything cooked for me at all?'

'Yes, I'll heat it up now,' she answered, and Sammy could see that she was eager to move off the topic of trouble. But though he discounted most of what Da said when he had been drinking, this time Sammy wasn't so sure. Tension was in the air, and something told him that his father might be right about blood on the streets. He hoped that he was wrong, but he felt a tiny shiver that told him otherwise.

'Hi there, popsters!' said Emma into the microphone, as she imitated the style of the disc jockeys she heard on the radio. 'We've got some groovy sounds for you tonight, but first, an interview with one of Belfast's coolest chicks, Maeve – the Rave – Kennedy!'

Sammy and Dylan burst out laughing, but even though Maeve was laughing too she put up her hands in protest.

'I can't do an interview, Emma, I wouldn't know what to say!'

'Say the first thing that comes into your head. Then it's more fun when we play the recording.'

It was Saturday night and they were in the living room of Goldmans' house. Emma's parents had dressed up to go for a meal in a posh restaurant, and Emma and Dylan had invited Maeve and Sammy to keep them company while their parents were out. In the last year or so they had persuaded their parents that they didn't need a babysitter any more, and Emma still loved this new freedom. Later her mother would drive Sammy and Maeve home, but for now they had a couple of hours without adult supervision, and

Emma was determined to make the most of it.

As soon as her parents had left she had taken out Dad's tape recording equipment. She would erase the tape later without telling him, and put everything back before he returned home, but right now she was enjoying making a mock programme.

Exaggerating her own American accent, Emma held the microphone out to Maeve. 'I'm here in the Belfast pad of rock star Maeve Kennedy. Put down that double whiskey, Maeve, and tell us about your new album.'

Maeve grinned and lowered her glass of lemonade. 'Well, we've just spent six months in the studio, and we think it's our best record yet.'

Emma was pleased that Maeve was entering into the spirit of things and she kept a straight face as she asked her next question: 'Are the rumours true that you're no longer writing songs with…' Emma hesitated briefly as she tried to think up a name for a rock star. 'With Ricky Romarro?'

'Ricky and I are still good friends,' answered Maeve without missing a beat. 'But we want to … we want to do our own material.'

Emma was impressed at how well Maeve had improvised and now she turned to Sammy and held out the microphone.

'So, artistic differences, ladies and gentlemen. Tell us your side of it, Ricky.'

'What?' said Sammy, taken by surprise.

'Sorry,' interjected Dylan. 'As Ricky's manager I don't want him talking to the press; he's been misquoted too often.'

Emma was glad to see her brother coming up with such a good line. He had seemed a bit preoccupied in the last couple of days, but this was more like his normal self.

'Ricky's fans have a right to know,' countered Emma. 'So tell us, Ricky. Has your time in LA caused a break-up with your writing partner, Maeve Kennedy?'

It was obvious that Sammy wasn't as natural an actor as Maeve, but he made an effort to sound convincing. 'Eh, Maeve and I … we've …we've made some good records together. And eh … well, just because we were on opposite sides of the Atlantic doesn't mean the band won't still tour.'

'But you're not writing together?'

'Not at the moment,' answered Sammy.

'And you no longer share a villa in Spain with Maeve Kennedy?'

'No comment, I must insist!' said Dylan.

Sammy shrugged as though his hands were tied. 'Sorry, that's personal. No comment.'

Emma could see that Maeve was knotted up with laughter at this turn in the conversation, and her mind went back to when her parents had left, and she and Dylan had been alone with Maeve and Sammy. Emma had detected a slight wariness between the other girl and boy. She remembered the argument about who had placed the reservoir bombs, and had decided to confront the matter of her friends' differing backgrounds.

'We ought to have a rule,' she had said.

Sammy had looked quizzical. 'What sort of rule?'

'A friends' rule. So we're not affected by all this stupid stuff that's going on around us.'

'What stuff?' asked Maeve.

'Politicians fighting each other. And Protestants looking down on Catholics, and Catholics hating Protestants. Let's have a rule that when we're together nobody's Jewish, or Catholic, or Protestant. We're just friends. And we leave the cranky stuff out of it. What do you say?'

Maeve nodded. 'I'll agree to that.'

'Sammy?'

Sammy seemed to consider it, then he too nodded. 'OK.'

'Great,' said Emma. 'Dylan?'

'What about Buddhists?' asked her brother, half seriously. 'Can we let Mom join if she stops being a Buddhist hippy?'

'Of course not, this is just for us. And we can make it a secret bond between us, like blood brothers.'

'Without the blood, please!' said Maeve.

Emma held out her hand. 'Let's all shake on it then.'

Each of the four reached out, and they all clasped hands.

That had been a few minutes earlier, and it had brought everyone closer and relaxed enough to record the joke radio programme. Now Emma continued in her role of interviewer, 'OK, folks, Ricky Romarro and Maeve Kennedy, still in the same band but not writing together. And selling their villa in Spain, according to our source. That's all for tonight, folks. This is Emma Goldman signing off from our Belfast studio.'

Emma switched off the recorder and looked at Sammy. 'So, enjoy your first recording?'

'Yeah. It was a bit mad, but I'm dying to hear it.'

'I bet I'll sound daft!' said Maeve.

Emma smiled, pleased that she had introduced Maeve and Sammy to their first tape recorder, and even more pleased that she had got everyone to agree to the secret bond.

'OK,' she said happily. 'Playback time!'

CHAPTER EIGHT

'What are you up to?' asked Emma.

Dylan didn't like lying to his sister, but he had no choice, so he kept his expression innocent-looking. 'Nothing.'

'So what's this secret thing you have to do in town?'

They were at the bus stop outside school, but instead of getting off at their stop on the Malone Road, Dylan had explained that he wanted to go on to the city centre.

'It's not a big secret,' he answered. 'I just need to do something.'

'Maybe I'll come on with you, then.'

'No. Sorry, Emma, I just …'

'You are up to something!'

Dylan held up his hands in surrender. 'OK. Look, I'm doing something I can't tell you about.'

'Is it something bad?'

'No!'

'So why can't you tell me about it?'

Because you'd tell Mom, Dylan thought to himself. Instead he made his voice as persuasive as possible. 'There's a reason, Emma. A good reason, but I can't tell you right now. Just trust me, OK?'

Emma looked at him appraisingly.

'Please,' he said.

'All right.'

Dylan felt relieved. 'Thanks, sis,' he said, then he held out his hand and flagged down the approaching bus, eager to be on his way.

Dylan sat hidden away in the furthest corner of the city library, not wanting to bump into anyone he knew. He had left Emma and travelled on to the city centre, alighting in Donegall Square. He had then walked the crowded pavements of Royal Avenue in the mild April sunshine, excited by the feeling of being on a secret mission.

And now he had succeeded in finding what he sought. Spread out on the library desk in front of him were books of instruction on the sport of boxing. He had been studying them intently and had made lots of notes, anxious to gain any possible advantage in the coming encounter with Gordon.

He had originally hoped that the trouble with Gordon might have died down and that the fight might be dismissed as something that had been proposed in the heat of the moment. Instead, Gordon had brought it up after the team's soccer match at the weekend. The gym that Gordon had suggested for their bout was being renovated, but Gordon had made it clear that he was looking forward to the fight when the gym reopened next week.

Dylan hadn't told Emma or his parents about the challenge, and with the other boy insisting on going ahead, there was no way out. But while Gordon was tough and had a bigger, heavier, build, he was also stupid. And boxing was a sport in which someone skilful and smart could beat a scrapper who relied on brute force.

Dylan looked again at his notes. He had no experience of boxing, but he was athletic, he had quick reactions, and he had learnt a lot about boxing techniques and tactics from the library books. Maybe he would give Gordon a surprise when they stepped into the ring. Buoyed by the thought, he returned to the books, eager to absorb every tip that might help in the fight.

Maeve felt scared when she saw the photograph on the front page of the Sunday newspaper. It showed a violent clash that had taken place during the rioting in Derry the previous day. A little over sixty miles was all that separated Belfast from Derry, so it seemed only a matter of time before trouble spread to Belfast.

It was a sunny morning, and Maeve and her aunt and uncle had left Mass in Clonard Monastery. Despite the warm spring air, Maeve felt chilled by the dramatic photographs that covered the front pages of all the newspapers that were on sale at the church gates. The civil rights movement was being violently opposed by some unionists, and things had become so bad that British troops were arriving later today to help support the police.

Growing up in Dublin, Maeve had never seen a riot. In the three years that she had lived in Belfast she had become used to the tension – and sometimes open hostility – between nationalists and unionists, but never before had she seen it turn into this kind of violence. But while the pictures from Derry were frightening, there were good developments too.

The twenty-one year old nationalist, Bernadette Devlin, had been elected to Westminster, making history as the youngest person ever to win a seat in parliament. Maeve had been pleased, partly because it was good to see a woman succeed but also because it meant change was possible, however much some people resented it. And there was to be a crucial vote on Tuesday night, when unionists were to decide on the issue of one-man-one-vote – one of the key demands of the civil rights campaign. It seemed obvious to Maeve that this was reasonable, but there was huge resistance to it, and it was uncertain how things would turn out.

'Uncle Jim?'

Yes, Maeve.'

'What happens if the one-man-one-vote-doesn't go ahead?'

'There'll be ructions.'

'Yeah?'

'More protest marches, more attacks on the marchers, all sorts of trouble.'

'I really hope they agree to it,' said Maeve.

'Then there'll be trouble on the other side,' pointed out Aunt Nan.

They turned the corner of the sunlit road and made for Bombay Street. Maeve normally would have been eager for the Sunday fry-up that Uncle Jim did after Mass, but today she wanted to question her aunt and uncle. 'Why are people so against the civil rights? What they're asking for is only fair.'

'That's life, Maeve,' said Uncle Jim gently. 'It's never been fair.'

'But shouldn't we try to change things so it is fair?'

Uncle Jim shrugged. 'The problem with change is that someone has to lose. If one group is getting the best jobs and the best houses, and then a fairer system is suggested, that first group will lose out.'

'But they'd only lose out on something that wasn't fair in the first place.'

'Tell that to Protestant workers in the shipyards if Catholics get employed.'

'So what are we supposed to do? Nothing?'

'Not nothing,' said Aunt Nan. 'But we can't be too impatient, Maeve, change takes time. If we start demanding our rights there'll be all sorts of trouble.'

Maeve was about to argue, but Aunt Nan held up her hand decisively. 'We pray for a better world, and eventually God hears our prayers. Meanwhile we get on with our lives, and don't get caught up in trouble. All right?'

'Right,' answered Maeve reluctantly. But it wasn't all right. Dad was serving with the UN peace-keepers in Cyprus, risking his life so that victims of the conflict there were protected and treated with justice. Yet back here in Ireland Aunt Nan was suggesting that people should accept injustice and not kick up too much of a fuss. The talk of Protestant workers made her think of Sammy, whose mother had a job in a mill and whose father had worked in a foundry before injuring his back. Maeve had grown to like Sammy, with his low-key, good natured manner. But why should his parents – or even Sammy himself – have first pick ahead of Catholics like Maeve and her family when it came to getting a job, or a house, or anything else? She said none of this to Aunt Nan, however, and walked on in silence.

'Ready for a plate of rashers and sausages?' asked Uncle Jim with a playful lilt in his voice.

Maeve knew that he meant well. 'Yes, please,' she answered, as enthusiastically as she could, but her worries hadn't really been addressed, and she sensed that there would be trouble ahead.

PART TWO

DEVELOPMENTS

CHAPTER NINE

Sammy wished that he had kept his mouth shut, but there was no going back now. His father stared angrily at him across the kitchen table. Florrie and Tess, the older two of his sisters, were doing their homework, and Ma, knowing the signs of trouble, turned to them.

'That's enough for now, girls; you can go out and play.'

'Thanks, Ma' said Florrie, and Sammy watched as his sisters immediately left the table and ran happily out to the street.

'Who the hell do you think you are?' said Da, looking Sammy in the eye.

'Bill,' said Ma placatingly.

'Don't "Bill" me!' he snapped.

Sammy had become an expert at gauging how much his father had drunk, and he calculated now that Da had enough taken to be aggressive, without being actually drunk.

'I was just saying, Da–'

'Don't say! I won't have a pup like you talking tripe. Giving me lip in my own home!'

Sammy had just heard on the radio that the Ulster Unionist Party had reluctantly agreed to change the voting system in Northern Ireland to allow one-man-one-vote. Even though Sammy was against the nationalists, who claimed to be Irish rather than

British, he thought that one-man-one-vote was only fair. His mistake, however, had been to say this to Da.

'What am I raising here, a bloody little Taig, is it!?'

'No, Da.'

'Next thing they'll be demanding jobs, and housing. Our jobs and our houses! Aye, and then it'll be joining the Irish Free State. Taking orders from Dublin and the Pope in Rome!'

Sammy said nothing, hoping that if Da got it all off his chest he might eventually calm down.

'And you, talking like a little traitor!' continued his father.

'He didn't mean anything by it, Bill,' said Ma.

'Didn't mean anything?! A bit of pressure and our politicians cave in, and he thinks that's OK?! Who's been poisoning your mind, sonny?' said Da, drawing closer. 'Who have you been listening to?'

'Nobody, Da,' Sammy answered, knowing that his father already disapproved of Dylan, and that if he knew about Maeve he would go berserk.

'Stand up when I'm talking to you!' said Da.

Sammy rose and could smell the beer on his father's breath as he drew in close to him. 'Do you want the Taigs taking over?'

'No, Da.'

'Do you want to be ruled by a crowd of bogtrotters in Dublin?'

'No, Da.'

'Do you want to be kissing bishops' rings and genuflecting before the Pope?'

'No, Da.'

Sammy kept his tone respectful and he hoped that his agreement to all the questions might satisfy his father. There was a pause as Da looked at him, as though weighing everything up.

'You need to decide which side you're on, sonny.'

'I'm on our side, Da.'

'So you've seen sense? That one-man-one-vote is a sell-out?'

The last thing Sammy wanted was to annoy his father. And all the other answers he had given him were true. But he couldn't bring himself to condemn one-man-one-vote.

'Well?'

Sammy could see Da's anger growing, yet something in him rebelled about being bullied into an outright lie. He hesitated, trying to find some way out, but before he could think of something his father lost his temper and smacked him in the face.

'No, Bill!' said Ma, quickly rising from her chair as Sammy staggered a little backwards.

It hadn't been a full force blow, but his face still stung, and he felt a surge of anger at his father. It must have shown in his expression because Da moved threateningly towards him.

'No!' cried Ma forcefully.

She stood directly in front of his father, her normal deference gone as she looked him in the eye. 'No,' she repeated.

Sammy saw his father hesitating, then Ma spoke again, without taking her eyes off her husband.

'Take your gear and go to training, Sammy. Now!'

Sammy moved quickly to grab his sports bag from the corner, then he crossed into the living room and out the hall door. He ran down the street, ignoring his sisters who called after him in farewell. Reaching the corner, he slowed down and gathered himself, trying to get his thoughts in order. It wasn't the first time that Da had hit him. And if Ma hadn't intervened it might have been a lot worse. Trying to look on the bright side, he was proud of himself for not caving in and saying something he thought was untrue. And things usually blew over quickly with Da, who sometimes tried to make up afterwards for his bad temper. Maybe this would be one of those times, Sammy hoped, as he felt his cheek, which was still a bit tender from the slap.

He crossed Tate's Avenue and his stinging face made him think of Dylan, and the beating he was likely to take by boxing an experienced and ruthless fighter like Gordon. The fight was scheduled for next week, and Sammy had been agonising about what he might do to save his friend. He had considered going to Buckie and asking him to intervene. But would Buckie do anything? He might think that a bout in the ring was an acceptable way for two boys to settle their differences. And even if Buckie did take action, Dylan might feel humiliated at having to be saved by the trainer. But then again being beaten around the ring and losing would also be humiliating. He wasn't sure what to do, and he reached the football ground and walked in the entrance gate, hoping to forget his worries for a while.

Emma tried not to get her hopes up too high. She had trained conscientiously since joining Ardara Harriers, and Mr Doyle had told her he was pleased with her progress. But would he pick her to enter the big under-thirteens' race that was coming up in a couple of weeks? Maeve claimed that he always gave runners plenty of notice, and both Emma and Maeve had made it their goal to compete for the club against some of the most promising young runners in Belfast. Training had gone well tonight, and Mr Doyle had asked to see the two girls. Surely he was going to give them his decision, Emma thought, as they walked across the grass running track, the lights of the city below them beginning to twinkle in the dusk.

'Hi, Mr Doyle, you wanted to see us,' said Emma cheerfully. Her mother was a great believer in the power of positive thinking. Dylan claimed that was all just hippy talk, but Emma wasn't so sure, and she hoped now that sounding confident might work in her favour.

Mr Doyle turned to her, his expression earnest and his eyes slightly bulging, as usual. 'Tell me this, Emma, what part of the States are you from?'

Emma was taken aback and she could see that Maeve was also surprised that the trainer wasn't talking about the forthcoming race. 'Eh … we lived in New York at first, and then in Washington.' she answered, not wanting to get into the rigmarole about not actually being from the States but being originally from England.

'Washington … it's a fine city, I'm told.'

'Yes.'

'I saw the news before I came out this evening,' continued Mr Doyle. 'And there was a piece from Washington.'

'Really?' said Emma, trying to sound fascinated, though in fact she had no idea where Mr Doyle was leading the conversation.

'They just announced that more American soldiers have died fighting in Vietnam than were killed in the Korean War.'

'Right …'

'It's a noble sacrifice in the fight against communism,' said Mr Doyle with a little approving nod. 'God Bless America, I say.'

Emma had seen the massive marches for peace in Washington and she knew that lots of Americans saw nothing noble about the war in Vietnam. She was really tired of people fighting each other, whether in Vietnam or here in Northern Ireland, but she didn't want to say the wrong thing to her trainer. She struggled to find the right response, then Maeve came to her rescue.

'Yeah, America's a great country. And it's produced lots of great runners, Mr D, hasn't it?'

Emma had to hold back a smile, so obvious was her friend's attempt to get the trainer onto the topic of running. If Mr Doyle realised that he had been dropped a hint, however, he gave no sign of it.

'It has indecd, Maeve,' he answered. 'And maybe the greatest athlete of them all in Jesse Owens. That lad put manners on Hitler at the Munich Olympics.'

Please, not another history lesson, thought Emma. Just tell us if we've been picked for the race!

'Right,' said Maeve, in eager agreement with Mr Doyle.

Emma looked at the trainer. Behind his odd appearance and unpredictable manner he was actually a nice man. And he had given her useful advice about her stride and on moving her arms less to preserve energy when running. But now she just wanted him to reveal whatever it was he had summoned them for. As if reading her mind, he coughed, then cocked his head to one side.

'I've been thinking about this under-thirteen race.'

'Yes?' said Emma, her heart starting to pound as she realised just how much she wanted to be picked.

'You're well ready for it, Maeve; I'm entering your name.'

'Thanks, Mr D.'

Emma felt her chest tighten. Did that mean he thought she wasn't ready for it? Surely even someone as odd as the trainer wouldn't be so cruel as to pick Maeve and then in the next breath dash her hopes.

'As for you, Emma, I've been watching you closely. Very closely. You've made good progress. You've taken on board what I've told you. But we still need to fine tune your stride.'

Emma's mouth had gone dry but she forced out the words. 'So, am I running in the race too?'

Mr Doyle looked at her as though surprised by the question.

'Oh yes. We've two weeks to do the fine tuning, so I'm entering you too.'

'Cool!'

'Right, that's settled so,' said Mr Doyle, then he gave a brisk nod and headed back across the running track

Emma turned to Maeve, who had a big grin on her face. 'That's brilliant, isn't it?'

'Yeah, it's great. Just one problem,' said Maeve, her face suddenly serious.

'What?'

'Will we still be friends when I beat you?!'

'Sure we will – cause you won't beat me! Race you back to the club house!' cried Emma, then she set off at speed, delighted at how things had worked out.

CHAPTER TEN

'**N**o mercy!' said Buckie, 'I want you to play the opposition off the pitch!'

Dylan liked the atmosphere of drama in the dressing room before a match, and today the coach had everybody hanging on his words.

'Last year these lads beat us on a dodgy penalty decision, so we owe them one. Get out there today and run them into the ground! Don't give them a minute to settle. Let them know that they're playing on our home ground, and that they're in for a pasting!'

With his tall, athletic build and his drooping moustache Buckie reminded Dylan of the gunslingers he had seen in Western movies. The coach stood commandingly at the entrance to the dressing room, the air heavy with the smell of wintergreen, and Dylan admired the way that Buckie could inspire the players. Every boy on the team would give his all today, partly for fear of the coach's disapproval, but mostly because the players wanted to please him.

'So, who are we?' asked Buckie.

'Wanderers!' cried the boys.

'And why are we here?'

'We're here to win!'

'All right then, go out and do it!'

There was a babble of excitement as the players headed for the door, but Dylan stopped when Buckie pointed at him. 'A quick word, son,' said the coach.

Dylan wondered if he had done something wrong. Surely if Buckie was dropping him he wouldn't wait until just before the team took to the pitch?

'You too, Gordon,' said the coach, and Gordon held back also, a look of enquiry on his face.

'I believe the pair of you are planning a scrap?' said Buckie.

Gordon went to speak, but the coach cut him off. 'Don't bother denying it. And don't argue with me, just button up and listen.'

Dylan was taken aback, but before he had time to get over his surprise Buckie continued.

'I'm not having this,' said the coach firmly. 'I've worked hard to build a raggle-taggle gang of young fellas into a team. You two aren't going to upset that and cause division. If you don't like one another you can knock lumps off each other in training. But you're not splitting my team into two camps. So put this fight out of your heads, it's not going to happen.'

Dylan couldn't believe his ears. Despite studying the books on boxing there was a good chance that he would get hurt by an experienced boxer like Gordon. And now, thanks to Buckie, there was a way out without losing face. Gordon looked put out by the coach's intervention, so Dylan made sure not to let any relief show on his face.

'Are we crystal clear on this?' asked Buckie. 'Dylan?'

'Yeah, OK.'

'Gordon?'

The other boy was still disappointed, but nobody would dare defy Buckie, and Gordon reluctantly nodded. 'Yeah, all right.'

'Good. Subject closed, I never want to hear about it again,' said the coach. 'Now get out there and take it out on the opposition. Go on!'

Dylan headed for the door, amazed at what had happened, and trying hard to keep a smile off his face.

'Sammy, you look like a boy who could knock back another Coke!' said Dylan's mother, looking enquiringly at Sammy across the table of the city centre Wimpy restaurant.

'Well …' said Sammy politely.

'"Well" definitely counts as a yes! And, Dylan, I don't have to ask you, do I?'

'That's right, Mom, you don't!'

'Damn the torpedoes, full steam ahead!' said his father with mock drama. 'Let's all have another.'

Dylan smiled as Dad called the waiter and ordered. He was happy to be here with his parents and Sammy, to mark the football team's victory. Emma was off at her ballet, but Dylan's parents had both come to see him playing in the game and had then invited Sammy along to the celebratory meal. The match had been a thrilling three-two victory for Wanderers, and Dylan had scored the second goal for his team.

All in all it had been a good day, starting with the unexpected cancelling of the fight by Buckie. It was something he would never have expected from the coach, and he wondered again how Buckie had heard about the boxing match. Of course, lots of the boys on the team had been talking about it, and it could have come to his attention that way. The other possibility was that Sammy had gone to him. If that were the case things were more complicated. Dylan couldn't deny that he was relieved not to have to fight Gordon. But he didn't like the idea of Sammy thinking he couldn't look after himself. Still, if it had been Sammy, he had been acting as a friend. Better to leave it for now and just enjoy the celebrations.

'You're a really good full back, Sammy,' said his mother now. 'You played very well today.'

'Thanks,' said Sammy modestly.

'No, I mean it. You've got real talent.'

Dylan had sensed Sammy being a bit overawed by his parents at first, but over time he had relaxed with them, and now he smiled.

'Well, sure you've talent too, haven't you? Dylan told me you're great at the painting.'

'My God! A son praising his mother! What next?!'

Sammy smiled. 'He said you're going to have – what do you call it – with the paintings?'

'An exhibition.'

'Yeah, an exhibition. And that your stuff is pretty good.'

'Wow! This could turn my head.'

Dylan lowered his hamburger and looked playfully at his mother. 'But to be fair, Mom, you're still terrible at telling jokes!' Dylan turned to his friend. 'You should have heard what we had to listen to on St Patrick's Day.'

'Here we go, reinforcements!' said Dad as the waiter arrived with a tray of drinks. He slipped the waiter a tip, then turned back to the others. 'And seeing as everyone else is ego-tripping, what wonderful things has Dylan told you about me?'

Even though Dad was obviously kidding, Dylan saw that Sammy felt he had to answer positively.

'He said the radio people love your work, and that you're planning a big story for the newspapers.'

Dad grinned wryly. 'I'm not sure about "loving" the work, but I'm in the right spot at the right time. The one-man-one-vote was a really big story, as you can imagine.'

'Yes,' answered Sammy, nodding agreement and looking suddenly serious.

'And there's more to come,' added Dad. 'It looks like the Prime Minister here is certain to resign. Great stuff for a newsman, though maybe not so good for Northern Ireland.'

'Do you think there'll be even more trouble?' asked Sammy.

'I'm afraid so.'

'But tonight's a night for celebration,' suggested Mom. 'So let's leave our worries aside.'

'Yeah,' agreed Dylan, glad that his mother had rescued the conversation from taking a gloomy turn.

'So,' she said brightly. 'What's on the lawn all summer in Ireland?'

'Aw, Mom.'

'Pattie O'Furniture! What do you call an American drawing? Yankee Doodle!'

'Mom!' cried Dylan, even though as he said it he was laughing. Dad might be right about trouble looming, but tonight he would enjoy himself, at the end of a surprising, eventful day.

CHAPTER ELEVEN

Maeve tore open the envelope excitedly. She was having breakfast with Uncle Jim and Aunt Nan, and the small kitchen was bright with early May sunshine. Already it was promising to be a beautiful day and the letter with the bright red Cypriot stamp had lifted her spirits further. Maeve loved hearing from her father, and his letters from the exotic location of Cyprus brought colour and excitement into her life.

'Great news!' she said, lowering the letter and looking to her aunt and uncle. 'Dad is coming home on leave!'

'Good,' said Uncle Jim, 'always delighted to see Mick.'

'Let's hope he doesn't bring you a bottle of the local firewater like last time,' said Aunt Nan, but though it sounded like a complaint, she said it with a smile, and Maeve knew that she would be pleased to see her brother again.

'He'll be back in Ireland for two weeks, it'll be brilliant!' said Maeve.

Although she got on really well with Aunt Nan and Uncle Jim, it was exciting when her father came home. Of course the down side was that it was sad when he had to go back, and sometimes Maeve wished that he didn't spend so much of his time overseas on UN peace-keeping duty.

He had explained to Maeve that it was an important job that

he was good at, and the only thing for which he was qualified. That had been several years ago when she had first gone to live in Belfast. Maeve had been upset at the time, but her father had revealed that he and Aunt Nan had been raised in an orphanage, and that they had made a vow that when they grew up they would take care of each other's children if anything ever happened to either of them. So when Maeve's mother had been killed in the car accident it was decided that she would live with Aunt Nan, and that Da would visit Belfast as often as his life as a soldier allowed.

Maeve thought it was strange now that he was serving with the Irish army as a peace keeper in Cyprus, when the peace here in Belfast was threatened by all the trouble that was brewing. But there was nothing she could do about any of that, so she would just enjoy spending time with her father. She would introduce him to her new friend, Emma, and she hoped he would like Emma as much as she liked Mr and Mrs Goldman.

'When is he coming home?' asked Aunt Nan.

'Later this month. It would be great if the weather stays good, we could all go on picnics,' said Maeve.

'I might be free for lots of picnics,' said Uncle Jim.

Maeve picked up on the downbeat tone of his voice and she looked at him. 'How do you mean?'

'Sorry, Maeve, that just slipped out. I don't mean to dampen your plans.'

'But what do you mean about being free for picnics?'

Uncle Jim hesitated, then shrugged. 'There's no point lying to you. They're talking about possible lay-offs in work.'

'Really?' said Maeve worriedly. Uncle Jim was a good carpenter and a conscientious worker, and it didn't seem fair that his job should be in danger.

'It might come to nothing,' said Aunt Nan. 'Business could pick up over the summer and everything might be fine.'

'I really hope so,' said Maeve.

'Nan is right,' said Uncle Jim brightly. 'Don't worry your head; it'll probably all work out fine.'

'Right,' agreed Maeve. But although she had made herself sound cheerful, and was still looking forward to seeing Da, a little of the good had gone out of the morning.

'Have you heard the latest, Sammy?' asked Da, a smile playing about his lips as he entered the kitchen.

It was Friday night, but Da hadn't gone out drinking yet, and for now he was good humoured and sober. It was over two weeks since the night when Sammy's father had slapped him in the face, and lately they had been getting on quite well. As often happened after Da lost his temper, he had seemed regretful the next day, and tried to make amends by being friendly. Sammy hadn't been sure how to respond. Part of him was relieved that Da was in better form, but part of him resented the fact that his father could lash out at him, then act as if it hadn't happened. If, one day, he got to study human behaviour, then maybe he would understand better. Usually, however, he went along if Da was in good spirits, so now he responded positively.

'No, Da, what's the latest?'

'St Christopher has been sacked! These Papists, they're a joke! All the Taigs with their St Christopher medals on the dashboards of their cars – wasting their time!' said Da with a laugh.

Sammy didn't know much about the Catholic religion but he had sometimes heard his father mocking the way Catholics had favourite saints to whom they prayed for favours. Even to a Protestant like Sammy, however, St Christopher was known for being the patron saint of travellers. It did seem strange that the Catholic Church was demoting someone whose face had appeared for years on the dashboards of countless cars, but Sammy had heard on the radio that the Church had dropped a whole series of people from its list of saints. 'How can you be a saint one day, and not be the next?' he asked.

'Exactly!' said Da with a grin. 'And what happened to all the prayers the Taigs said to St Christopher, now it turns out he wasn't a saint?!'

Sammy smiled, even though he didn't fully share Da's disdain for Catholics, especially since he had become friendly with Maeve. Wanting to distract his father from the topic, he posed a different kind of question. 'What's going to happen now we've a new Prime Minister, Da?'

After the one-man-one-vote was very narrowly passed by the

Unionist Party, Terence O'Neill had resigned as Prime Minister of Northern Ireland, to be replaced by James Chichester-Clarke. Sammy didn't know if this would improve matters or make them worse, but he saw at once that his father was unimpressed by the change.

'It won't do anything for us. Chichester-Clarke,' said Da derisively, rolling the double barrelled name on his lips. 'A lot he cares about folks like us!'

Sammy was sorry now that he had brought politics into it and changed Da's mood. His mother and sisters had gone out for a walk, however, so there was nobody else here to lighten things.

'Would you say Mr Chichester-Clarke carried a St Christopher medal, Da?' he said jokingly.

He was rewarded with a wry smile from his father. 'He might be an upper-class twit, but at least he's more cop-on than the Taigs.' His father suddenly flicked his head as though dismissing a topic that was beneath him. 'Anyway, I'm going down to The Grapes for a few pints. Tell your ma I'll be back about nine for my dinner.'

'OK, Da,' answered Sammy, as his father nodded and made for the front door.

The talk about religion made Sammy aware again of how angry his father would be if he knew about Maeve. It was bad enough in Da's eye that he was friends with Dylan. Had it not been for Ma insisting that they needed the fees paid by Mr Goldman, Da would probably have banned him from being friends with a boy who was both Jewish and middle class.

Thinking of Dylan, his mind went back to Buckie stopping the boxing match. Did Dylan suspect that he had gone to the trainer and tipped him off? In the last couple of weeks Dylan had never mentioned it, and Sammy hoped that he never would. He wasn't sorry that he had acted to save his friend from a beating, though he feared Dylan might be angry that he had gone behind his back. But what else could he have done? And if Dylan asked him outright, should he lie? Could he lie? He didn't know, and he hoped he wouldn't have to find out.

CHAPTER TWELVE

Emma accelerated when she heard the bell sounding for the final lap of the race. She was at the back of the leading group of four runners who had pulled ahead of the rest of the field. Time to make her move. Ahead of her in third place was Maeve, in second place was Lucy Coyle, the girl who had tripped her that first night in Ardara Harriers ground, while the leading runner was a dark-haired girl from a running club in Stranmillis.

Maeve was making her move also, and was starting to overtake Lucy Coyle on the outside. Emma had learnt her lesson the last time, and she was ready for any dirty tactics from the other girl as she tucked in behind Maeve.

Sure enough, Lucy tried to elbow Maeve as she went past her, but Maeve blocked her with her elbow, then forged ahead. Increasing her pace to keep up with Maeve, Emma drew level with Lucy Coyle. This time, however, she didn't wait for Lucy to try to elbow or trip her. Instead, Emma took the other girl by surprise, giving her a quick jab with her elbow as she powered past her.

For a brief moment Emma exulted in having paid back Lucy Coyle, then she concentrated again on the two runners in front of her. Maeve had closed the gap on the leading girl, and as they neared the next bend Emma saw her friend speed up again to overtake the runner from Stranmillis.

Emma could hear the roars of the spectators, with Mr Doyle's unmistakeable voice to the fore as he urged on his two competitors. Normally Emma could count on the support of her family too, but tonight Dad was covering a civil rights meeting and Mom had taken Dylan to his soccer training. Not that Emma needed her family present in order to be motivated. She really wanted to win this race and show Mr D that the time he had spent refining her running technique hadn't been in vain.

The girl from Stranmillis tried to accelerate after Maeve, but Emma sensed that the dark-haired girl had little more to give, and as they came around the bend she overtook her. Maeve was about a yard ahead, but Emma felt strong, and she gave another spurt that brought her to just behind her friend's shoulder.

She was aware of how much Maeve wanted to win this race, and it seemed a pity that one of them had to be disappointed. If it hadn't been for Maeve she wouldn't have joined Harriers, wouldn't have met Mr Doyle, and probably wouldn't have improved to the point where she had a real chance to win. Still, now they were competing with each other, and one of them had to succeed at the expense of the other.

She sensed that Maeve's pace was slackening ever so slightly, and she accelerated again. To her delight she found herself level with her friend. Now they were approaching the final bend, and the cheering was reaching a crescendo. Emma could see the finish line in the distance and although her chest was pounding as she gulped in air, it was as if time slowed down in these final moments. She saw Maeve glancing over at her as they drew level, and even in that glimpse she recognised the fear in Maeve's eyes that victory could be snatched from her.

Emma felt a stab of guilt, knowing that it was Maeve's friendliness and generosity that had drawn her into Ardara Harriers. And although Emma got on fairly well with the other girls in school, she hadn't become close to any of them the way she had with Maeve. Would it put their friendship in jeopardy now if she won a race that she knew Maeve desperately wanted to win? And was winning worth more than their friendship? On the other hand, a real friend wouldn't hold it against you if you won fair and square. Would she?

They sprinted neck and neck into the home straight. Emma suddenly dismissed all thoughts from her mind and simply ran flat out. She felt herself drawing ahead of Maeve, then the finishing line seemed to be flying towards her and she thundered across the line, raising her arms exultantly in victory.

Mr Doyle ran onto the track, his face creased with a smile as he gave her a hug, '*Maith an cailín*, Emma! *Maith an cailín*!'

'Thanks, Mr D!' she said delightedly.

She turned round to seek out Maeve and she could see at once the disappointment on her friend's face.

'Well done, Emma,' Maeve said, offering her hand.

Emma reached out and shook it. 'Thanks, Maeve, and well done coming second.'

Maeve tried for a smile but looked crestfallen, and Emma sensed that she had said the wrong thing.

'I'm just going to get my top, see you in a bit,' said Maeve, before turning away and making for the changing room.

Emma's delight at winning the race was fading, and she wondered if she had made an error in coming into Harriers as the new girl and winning a race that meant so much to her friend. But wouldn't a friend worth having accept that in a race the fastest girl ought to win?

She saw Mr Doyle approaching again, his face still wreathed in a smile. She smiled in return, telling herself that everything with Maeve would work out. Yet in her moment of victory, she couldn't help but feel a little deflated.

'Dylan, hang on a second, will you?'

Dylan stopped, surprised by the friendly tone of Gordon's voice. It was a sunny evening in May, and Wanderers had just drawn an exciting match with a team from Woodvale. All the other boys were making for the Nissen hut that served as the pavilion, but Dylan hung back now, curious to see what Gordon wanted.

It was three weeks since Buckie had stopped their boxing match. The other boys on the team accepted that the trainer had intervened, and nobody had blamed either Dylan or Gordon for the fight being cancelled. But although they hadn't fought, they hadn't made peace either, and Gordon had been as unfriendly as ever.

So what was going on now? Maybe the other boy had decided that it would be better for Wanderers if everyone on the team got on together and played for each other. And if Gordon was willing to let bygones be bygones then Dylan would do the same.

'Yeah?' he said encouragingly

'I need to tell you something,' said Gordon, drawing nearer. 'In private.'

'OK,' answered Dylan, and he remained on the pitch as the other boys began to enter the pavilion.

Gordon waited until everyone was out of earshot, then he turned to Dylan and looked him in the eye. 'You better stop trying to show me up,' he said.

Dylan was taken aback. Now that there was no-one around, Gordon had dropped the friendly tone and spoken aggressively.

'What are you talking about?' Dylan asked.

'All these fancy runs you're doing. Up and down the wing, in and out of the box, who do you think you're impressing?'

'Well, Buckie for one, seeing as he picks me each week!' snapped Dylan, annoyed that Gordon's earlier tone had just been used to fool anyone overhearing him.

'It's not your job to waltz in and out of the box,' said Gordon, 'I'm the centre forward.'

'What are you afraid of – that I might score more goals?'

'I'm not afraid of anything, but you should be.'

'Should I?'

'You better back off and let me play the way I always have.'

'You play your way, I'll play mine,' said Dylan.

'No, you won't. I'm sick of you showing off and getting in my way. You better cut it out if you know what's good for you.'

Dylan felt his anger rising. 'Or what?' he said.

Gordon drew nearer, his voice low and threatening. 'Or you might have an accident in training. Last year Robbie Musgrave broke his leg on the training ground. Awkward tackle. He was in plaster for six weeks and out of the game for eight months.'

Dylan felt a chill run down his spine at the thought, but he was careful not to show any fear. 'You won't bully me,' he said.

'Yeah? Going to run squealing to Buckie again?'

'I never went to Buckie last time!'

'Really?'

'Yeah, really.'

'Someone did.'

'Not me.'

'Then how did he know about the boxing match?'

'You set it up in a room full of people. Anyone could have yapped about it.'

'Like your little pal Sammy. Did he save your yellow skin?'

Dylan hesitated, trying to come up with a retort. But the problem was that Sammy *might* have gone to Buckie.

'Doesn't matter,' continued Gordon. 'Everyone knows I'd have beaten you. And don't bother squealing to Buckie again, I'll deny everything.'

Gordon drew closer till their faces were almost touching, then he spoke menacingly. 'Tell anyone about this and you'll end up in plaster. And no-one will ever prove it wasn't an accident. Do the smart thing if you know what's good for you.'

Gordon turned away and walked off, and Dylan stood on the pitch, a bit shaken and unsure what to do.

CHAPTER THIRTEEN

'**F**air play to you, Maeve,' said Mr Doyle, 'you unearthed a good one in Emma!'

'Yeah …'

'A cracking runner. And you did well yourself. Only half a yard behind her, to give Harriers first and second place – well done.'

'Thanks, Mr D,' said Maeve, 'it was great for the club.'

It was the week after the race and they were standing on the running track before training began. Maeve felt a little nervous about meeting Emma tonight. She had been really disappointed in the aftermath of the race and, looking back, she realised that she should have congratulated Emma more on her win. Then last weekend she had travelled to Strabane to visit Uncle Jim's relations, and she hoped that Emma wouldn't think that she had been sulking and avoiding her.

'Talk of the devil!' said Mr Doyle now.

Maeve looked around to see Emma approaching them.

'Hi, Mr Doyle,' she said.

'Emma, *maith an cailín.*'

'Hi, Maeve.'

'Emma.' Maeve felt slightly uncomfortable.

Mr Doyle briskly clapped his hands. 'All right, girls, timed sprints in ten minutes. Don't forget your stretching.'

'OK, Mr D,' said Maeve as the trainer headed off to the far side of the track. Maeve hesitated, then decided to take the plunge. 'I'm … I'm sorry about last week, Emma.'

'Sorry for what?'

'For … for not behaving better when you won. I wanted that medal, but you won fair and square. I should … I should have been nicer,' she finished awkwardly.

Emma looked at her, and Maeve hoped the other girl would accept her apology. To her surprise, Emma grinned.

'What?'

'I would have been the same if it was my club and a new member got a medal I wanted.'

'Yeah?'

'Probably worse!'

Maeve smiled, relieved at this unexpected turn of events. 'So we're friends?'

'Of course.'

'And I wasn't sulking at the weekend. I really had to go away to Strabane.'

'No problem. How was it?'

'Kind of boring,' answered Maeve, 'meeting all these old uncles and aunts. It would have been far more fun making radio programmes with you.'

'Talking of radio programmes, Dad found out I've been using his tape recorder.'

'Oh no.' Maeve looked nervously at Emma. 'Did he find the

recording we made? '

'No, I rubbed that out. But he knew I'd been using the equipment.'

'Did he go mad?'

'No. I thought he might, but he was kind of cool.'

'What did he say?'

'Not to go behind his back again.'

'Right.'

'But he said I should make a proper programme.'

Maeve looked at her friend in surprise. 'Really?'

'He suggested a short documentary.'

'On what?'

'Anything I like. We could work on it together if you want?'

'Yeah! Brilliant! Would my name be mentioned at the end?'

'Of course. Co-produced by 'Maeve the Rave' Kennedy!' said Emma in her mock dramatic voice. 'So will we think something up, and give it a go?'

'Definitely.'

'Great. Now we better get stretching or Mr Doyle will be on the warpath.'

'OK, stretching it is,' said Maeve happily, excited by the idea of a radio programme, and glad they were still good friends.

Sammy hoped that there wasn't going to be a row. He was sitting at the kitchen table with his father and Mr Goldman, and he recognised the signs that Da's anger was simmering. Normally Ma made a point of being present when Dylan's father called to the house in his role as a journalist. She would always serve tea and try to keep the atmosphere pleasant, but tonight she was tending to a neighbour who had taken ill. Sammy guessed that Mr Goldman was smart enough to know that Da resented his presence in their home. Journalists needed first hand local information, however, and clearly Mr Goldman was prepared to put up with some hostility to get the views of a working-class Protestant family. And in fairness to Mr Goldman, he was always polite and agreeable, even when Da's manner was surly. Sammy and Dylan being friends through the soccer club should have made things easier, but instead Da took exception to being paid by the father of his son's friend.

Dylan's father was always discreet in his handling of the payment. Sammy suspected that Mr Goldman sensed Da's discomfort, and so was at pains to ensure that it didn't look like a handout, but instead was presented as a professional fee. It even came in a sealed envelope with a typewritten address. Despite all this, Sammy could see that Da's resentment was rising now.

'More tea, Mr Goldman?' Sammy asked, hoping to ease the tension.

Dylan's father smiled at him but shook his head. 'No thanks, Sammy, I'm fine.'

'Or some more brack?'

'If he wanted more brack he'd help himself, Sammy!'

'Sorry, Da,' said Sammy, not wanting to do anything to make matters worse.

'Thanks for the offer, Sammy,' said Mr Goldman. 'It's delicious brack, but I'm trying to count the calories these days.'

Once more he smiled, and Sammy couldn't help but wonder why Da couldn't be more like Mr Goldman? OK, he hadn't a well-paying, interesting job, and he hadn't been to college like Dylan's dad, but surely you didn't have to be wealthy or well educated to be polite? Sammy felt guilty for thinking ill of his father, but he couldn't help it.

'So, Bill,' said Mr Goldman, turning back to Sammy's father. 'To return to what I was saying. Of course I take your point that working-class Protestants have suffered harsh conditions for years. But what about the view that they should blame their political masters, rather than fellow workers who happen to be Catholic?'

'What are you suggesting? We should be friends with a crowd of Papists?'

'I'm not actually suggesting anything,' said Mr Goldman. 'I just want to know your view.'

'I've nothing in common with Taigs. I'm a loyal Ulsterman; I stand for Queen and country. They're a crowd of traitors who kow-tow to the Pope and want us in the Irish Free State!'

'And the fact that working-class people of both camps want better working conditions and better housing?'

'I don't give a fiddlers about their housing or working conditions!

Let the government improve conditions for us, the people loyal to the Crown, loyal to Ulster!'

Sammy thought that there was no point getting angry with Mr Goldman, who was only asking questions as part of his job. The journalist was calmly writing down Da's responses in shorthand, but Sammy could tell that his father somehow blamed Mr Goldman for raising the issue of both Catholics and Protestants suffering poor conditions in many areas of Belfast.

'Put that in your newspaper! Aye, and you can say that Bill Taylor said it!'

'Thank you for your frankness, but my sources remain anonymous.'

'Your sources?' said Da derisively, and Sammy sensed that his father's ugly mood was such that he was eager now to pick a fight. As though aware of this, Mr Goldman clicked shut the point of his pen and put away the paper on which he had been writing.

'I think we'll leave it at that for now. Thank you, Bill, as ever, for your honesty. And thank you, Sammy, for the tea and brack.'

'You're welcome,' said Sammy, as the journalist rose.

'And my best wishes to your mother.'

'Thanks, I'll tell her,' said Sammy, rising to compensate for the fact that Da had rudely remained sitting at the table.

'Cheerio, Bill,' said Mr Goldman.

'Bye,' said Da, curtly.

Sammy saw Mr Goldman to the door, where the older man shook hands warmly.

'Goodbye, Sammy, and we look forward to seeing you at the next barbecue, if not sooner.'

'Thanks, Mr Goldman. All the best.'

The visitor nodded in farewell, then stepped out the front door. Sammy knew that he didn't park his fancy car on their street, but left it instead up on Tate's Avenue, not wanting to draw attention to his being with the Taylor family. But his discretion counted for nothing now, and Da sneered when Sammy turned to the kitchen.

'Thank you, Mr Goldman! All the best, Mr Goldman!'

Sammy was hurt by his father's mimicry. 'I was only being polite,' he said.

'What are you making out?! That I wasn't?!'

The smart thing would be to back down now, but his father had been rude – really rude.

'I'm talking to you, sonny,' said Da.

'I know,' snapped Sammy. 'I was nice 'cause you weren't!' Sammy didn't know how he had found the courage to tell the truth, and now his father rose and rounded the table, making for him

'Don't you give me lip, boy!'

'I'm not, Da,' said Sammy. 'But I haven't done something wrong by being polite.' Sammy half expected a blow but he wasn't going to back down now, and he would take a beating if necessary.

Instead Da mocked him again. 'More brack, Mr Goldman! More tea, Mr Goldman. What were you like?!'

'Ma always taught us to be polite, and to make guests welcome. I was only doing what she said.'

His father stared at him, but Sammy sensed that Da found it hard to challenge the training that Ma had drilled into all her children.

'Just because your mother wants Goldman's money doesn't mean we've to dance attention on him. He's not a normal guest. He's not a friend.'

Sammy wanted to answer that his son Dylan was his friend, but he said nothing for fear that Da might then ban him from seeing the other boy. And that would be worse than a beating. Although he had other friends on his road with whom he played football, and kick the can, and other street games, his friendship with Dylan had opened up a more glamorous and exciting world. He couldn't bear to have that snatched away. But there was a real danger now that in a flash of anger his father might ban him from seeing Dylan. He had to win Da over, and he swallowed hard, then spoke in a conciliatory tone. 'I'm sorry if I sounded cheeky, Da. I didn't mean to.'

His father looked at him for what seemed an age, then he nodded. 'All right. We'll let it go this time. Clear up the table here, then do your homework.'

'Yes, Da,' said Sammy, secretly angry at the injustice of it all, but relieved nonetheless that he had probably just saved a friendship.

CHAPTER FOURTEEN

Maeve felt a thrill as the train sped across the estuary at Malahide. The sun sparkled on the dancing waves of the broad stretch of water and, looking out the carriage window, she couldn't see the bridge that carried the railway, so that it seemed like the train was magically suspended while crossing the shimmering blue sea.

She was excited also to be meeting her father, who had arrived back in Ireland last night on an army flight from Cyprus to Dublin. He would be coming up to Belfast to spend most of his holidays with Maeve, but she had persuaded Aunt Nan to let her travel the one hundred and six miles to Dublin to greet him. It meant that they could have a couple of days together in Dublin and that Maeve could be reunited, if only briefly, with friends from her native city.

Maeve had accepted that Belfast was her home now. Her Dublin friends kidded her about how she had picked up the Northern accent, but part of her would always be a Dubliner, and she was looking forward to shopping in Henry Street with her father this afternoon, and maybe visiting Dublin Zoo tomorrow.

This was the first time that she had made the train journey alone between Belfast and Dublin. It had taken a bit of persuading, but eventually she had convinced Aunt Nan and Uncle Jim that at twelve years of age she was capable of travelling by herself for a couple of hours. Nevertheless her aunt and uncle had accompanied her to Great Victoria Street Station, instructed her not to talk to strangers, and seen her onto the Enterprise, the gleaming diesel train that ran between the two cities. Aunt Nan had given her wrapped ham sandwiches, two slices of apple tart, and a bottle of milk with a screw cap, all of which made Maeve feel like she was setting off on an adventure.

She had brought along her Enid Blyton book, *The Secret of Moon Castle*, and later a boy of about seventeen had joined her carriage at Dundalk, bringing with him a transistor radio tuned to Radio Luxembourg. Obeying her aunt's instruction not to talk to strangers, Maeve hadn't spoken to him, but she had happily sung under her breath when two of her favourite songs, 'Jumping Jack Flash' and 'Ob-La-Di, Ob-La-Da', were played on the transistor radio.

Now Maeve felt her pulses starting to race a little as the train sped through the suburbs of Dublin, making its way towards Connolly Station, where she was to meet her father. She loved reunions with him, and he always brought her some kind of present from his travels abroad. But she was usually a little nervous too. Apart from the risk of him being killed or injured, Maeve was conscious that things could change when people were apart. Supposing he met someone and wanted to get married again? Would she be expected to leave Aunt Nan and Uncle Jim and live with a stepmother? She was probably worrying needlessly, she reasoned, and Dad had said nothing about any other woman, but still there was always a trace of anxiety until they were reunited and got back into their usual routine.

Maeve felt the train slowing as it approached Connolly Station and for some reason she found herself slightly more on edge than usual. Maybe it was the unsettling effect of the trouble that seemed to be spreading in Northern Ireland. Or the fact that Uncle Jim's job was under threat, despite him putting on a brave face. But for whatever reason she wanted the reassurance of everything feeling right, as it usually did when she saw her father.

Before she could consider it any more the train came to a halt and everyone in the carriage gathered their belongings. The boy with the transistor radio was doing a funny walk to the strains of 'Israelites'. This was a new song that had introduced Maeve to reggae. There had been great fun in school when one of the girls had misheard a line in the song as 'Get up in the morning, baked beans for breakfast,' but now Maeve was impervious to the catchy melody, and she gathered her bag and quickly alighted onto the platform.

She headed for the busy concourse, the air scented with diesel fumes, and she showed her ticket to the collector. Suddenly she saw a smiling figure bearing down on her. It was Dad, looking tanned and fit and with a huge smile on his face.

'Where's my girl?' he cried.

Maeve ran to him, and he swept her up off the ground and swung her, like he used to when she was small. Maeve laughed, and he swung her around some more before gently setting her down.

'It's great to see you, pet,' he said.

'It's brilliant to see you too, Dad,' answered Maeve. To her surprise her eyes suddenly filled up with tears, yet everything somehow seemed right as she stood there, happily wrapped in the arms of her father.

'Are you sure you want to do this?' whispered Dylan.

Sammy nodded. 'No going back.'

They were in the changing room after a drawn soccer match against a team from Dundonald, and Dylan thought his heart was racing faster now than it had during the match. Some members of the team had already departed, and others were joking and chatting and packing their kit. Dylan tried not to show any anxiety, but he had been tense all through the match, and now he felt nervous, knowing that a showdown was at hand.

A couple of days ago he had asked for Sammy's advice regarding Gordon's threat to break his leg. Sammy had thought about it, and said that they should sort this out themselves. Dylan wasn't sure this was the right way to handle a bully, but Sammy insisted that it would be better not to involve any adults. Sammy had made no reference to Buckie banning the boxing match, and Dylan had decided to leave well enough alone, and not ask his friend if he had told the trainer.

Sammy had then come up with a plan that was frighteningly simple, and Dylan had ignored Gordon's threat today and played his normal game in the drawn match. But he knew that Sammy was right, and that they needed to act before Gordon got a chance to carry out his threat at the next training session.

Dylan and Sammy had deliberately changed slowly after today's game, so that they would be among the last to leave, and now as Gordon rose to depart, Sammy spoke. 'Can you hang on a minute, Gordon? Me and Dylan want a word.'

Gordon looked at Sammy coolly. 'Really?'

'Yeah. Can you give us a few minutes alone, lads?' said Sammy to the few other players still present.

Dylan could see that the other boys were burning with curiosity, but they agreed to Sammy's request, took up their kit bags and left.

'What's this about?' said Gordon aggressively.

Sammy was about to answer, but Dylan held up his hand. 'Let me tell him,' he said, pleased at how steady his voice sounded. Now that the moment had arrived he felt a certain recklessness and he knew instinctively that he needed to take the upper hand with Gordon. 'First things first,' Dylan said, crossing to the dressing room door and turning the key in the lock, then popping the key into his pocket.

He saw the look of surprise on Gordon's face.

'Don't want you running away before we're finished with you,' said Dylan. 'Oh, and don't worry about Buckie coming back, he's gone off on duty with the Specials. We won't be disturbed till the caretaker comes round.'

'What do you think you're at?' demanded Gordon.

'It's about maths, really,' said Dylan.

'What?'

'You look too much of a numbskull to be good at maths, but I'll keep it simple.'

'You watch your mouth, pal!' said Gordon threateningly.

But Dylan had worked himself into a state of fearlessness now and he shook his head.

'No, I don't think I will. I'm done trying not to offend you. So, are you good at maths?'

'Look—'

'No, probably not. So I'll do the sums for you. There's one of you and two of us. On your own you could really hurt one of us. Even two-against-one, you'll probably hurt us a bit. But not as much as we'll hurt you. No matter how hard you fight, you'll lose in the end. And that's when we'll beat a lesson into you.'

Dylan saw Gordon look disbelievingly at him before turning to Sammy.

'Sammy?'

'Shut up and listen,' said Sammy.

'What, afraid of a fair fight, are you?' said Gordon.

'Fair?' said Dylan. 'You don't know the meaning of the word. Was it fair when you beat up Jimmy Gannon? Or picked on me, or anyone else you don't like? The only time you care about fairness is when it's against you. So hard luck – it's your turn tonight.'

Dylan deliberately took off his watch, and Sammy removed his sweater in an arranged move designed to intimidate Gordon with their readiness for battle. Dylan watched the bigger boy carefully. He sensed that the threat of the two of them beating him into submission had registered.

'You've no-one to blame but yourself,' said Sammy. 'But it doesn't have to be like this.'

'What do you mean?'

'We're here to give you a hiding. But if you swear on the Bible that breaking Dylan's leg won't happen, we'll let you go.'

'You'll let me go?!' said Gordon.

'Yeah. Otherwise we'll beat the lard out of you.'

Dylan could see that despite Gordon's attempted bluster, for once the other boy was unsure of himself.

'Not so nice on the receiving end, is it?' asked Dylan.

'I'll get each of you on your own!' said Gordon threateningly

'No,' answered Sammy calmly, 'you won't. After the hiding we give you, you won't look crooked at either of us again. And other people won't be so scared of you either, when they hear we put manners on you.'

'And once we start, there's no stopping,' added Dylan. 'Halfway through a hiding you can't cry halt and agree to swear. You swear now, or you take everything that's coming. Your choice.'

Dylan guessed that in years of bullying Gordon had never had the tables turned on him before, and that while the other boy was taking their threat seriously, he didn't want to lose face.

'You were stupid to get yourself into this,' said Sammy. 'Are you going to stay stupid? Or are you going to swear?'

Gordon said nothing and Sammy pointed his finger at him. 'I won't ask you again.'

Still the other boy gave no answer.

'OK, let's do it!' said Dylan. He clenched his fists, took a deep breath and started toward Gordon. Sammy advanced at the same time, and Gordon retreated instinctively.

'All right!' he cried. 'All right, I'll swear!'

Dylan halted, taking care not to show any relief. 'OK, Sammy,' he said, 'let's have your bible.'

Sammy took a King James Bible from his kitbag and handed it over. Dylan took the book and held it out in front of Gordon.

'All right, big shot,' he said, unable to keep the satisfaction from his voice, 'Time to take your oath.'

Emma took the stairs two steps at a time, eager to get out of school. Next month they would be breaking up for summer, and she was counting the days. In fairness, her Belfast school was co-educational, not too strict, and certainly not the worst of the many places in which she had been educated during her family's travels. But today she was frustrated with her classmates, and she quickly made for the entrance gate, where she had arranged to meet Dylan.

During break Emma had told several of her fellow pupils about her plans to make a radio documentary. Maybe it had been a mistake to expect them to be as keen as Maeve, but Emma had been surprised at the response. Instead of regarding it as an adventure, the general view seemed to be that it was a weird thing to do, and that something as boring as making radio programmes was best left to adults. Emma couldn't believe their attitude and had wanted to scream at them that it was they who were boring, but instead she hid her disappointment.

Now she saw Dylan standing in the sunshine just inside the school gate, and he smiled as she approached.

'Hi, Sis.'

'Hi.' Since his match yesterday Dylan had been in good form, although Emma didn't know why, seeing as the game had been a one-all draw and he hadn't scored. 'What has you so pleased?' she asked.

'Bonzo let us out of history a few minutes early. What has you so cross?'

'Just … the whole place,' said Emma with a shrug as they left the school and made for the bus stop.

'It's not the worst school.'

'It's not just the school. It's the school, the tennis club, Belfast. Everywhere we go we seem to be … I don't know … on the edge, looking in.'

'I know,' said Dylan sympathetically. 'We're always the new kids.'

'I'm tired of being the new kids. I'm tired of just starting to break in, and then moving somewhere else.'

'It's better than when we moved to New York first. And it's been pretty good with Sammy and Maeve.'

'Yeah, they've been great,' admitted Emma.

'Look, I know it's hard to feel good about moving, like Dad said. But he kind of has a point.'

'How's that?'

'Moving is the bad part of his job. But there's lots of good parts too. And we get all of those. I've been trying to see it that way.'

Emma was surprised by her brother being so philosophical. 'What brought that on?' she asked.

'Maybe it was thinking about Sammy and his psycho father. Or even Maeve, living with her aunt and uncle because her mom's dead.'

Emma knew that Maeve would be coming back to Belfast with her father tonight, and although he sounded nice, and Emma was looking forward to meeting him, she felt that it must be strange to have your father living in another part of the world.

'Mom and Dad aren't too bad really, when you look around,' said Dylan.

'I know,' conceded Emma. She smiled wryly. 'If Dad would just get a job in one place, and Mom was less of a hippy, they'd be perfect.'

'Still. Mom's exhibition next month will be fun.'

'Yeah. Do you think we could ask Maeve and Sammy along?'

Dylan frowned. 'Not as kids on their own. But we could ask Mom to invite their families.'

'We could, couldn't we?' said Emma, excited by the idea. 'I'd love to meet Sammy's psycho dad!'

'And Maeve's aunt, who thinks of herself as a personal friend of Saint Anthony!'

Emma laughed. 'Do you really think they'd come?'

'Why not? Sammy's dad can go for the free drink, and Maeve's aunt might convert a few Jews!'

Emma laughed again, her spirits lifted by her brother's irreverence.

'So, end of school and Mom's exhibition to look forward to,' said Dylan. 'Roll on June.'

Emma smiled and nodded in agreement. 'Roll on June!'

CHAPTER FIFTEEN

Maeve couldn't remember the last time she felt so happy. She looked out across the high peaks of the Mountains of Mourne and breathed in the sweet country air. It was just over halfway through her father's two weeks of leave, and she had enjoyed every day of it. Last weekend they had shopped in Dublin, visited old friends and neighbours in Harold's Cross and had Sunday lunch at Dublin Zoo. Early next morning they had travelled together to Belfast and each day after school Dad had something lined up for them to do. They had picnicked on Cave Hill, gone swimming at Donaghadee, listened to a band recital in Dunville Park and gone to see *Hello Dolly* in the cinema.

Best of all, though, was today, Whit Monday, when Dad had offered to take some of Maeve's friends up the mountains for a day trip. Maeve had invited Emma, Dylan and Sammy, and Dad had driven them in his hired car from Belfast to Newcastle, before ascending into the scenic heights of the Mourne Mountains. They had had a sing-song in the car, with Dylan leading a boisterous version of the recent hit 'Lily the Pink'. Sammy had brought along his mouth organ, and even Dad had joined in the singing when Sammy played 'It's a Long Way to Tipperary' and 'Pack up your Troubles'.

Maeve was pleased that her friends had clearly taken to Dad, who had the knack of getting everyone to enter into the adventures he planned without sounding too bossy.

'OK', he said now, 'I've a question for you all, and a bar of chocolate for whoever gets it right.'

They had been taking a break after a steep climb to a spectacular viewing point, but now Maeve's friends turned away from the vista of the surrounding peaks and the distant blue of the sea.

'The Mourne Wall,' said Dad, pointing. 'Amazing, isn't it?'

Maeve looked at the wall that snaked out across the surrounding mountain slopes, its granite stone glinting in the summer sunshine. It was almost five feet high and nearly three feet thick and it did look amazing as it seemed to stretch off into infinity.

'Built by hand over fifty years ago,' said Dad. 'Can you imagine the back-breaking work involved?'

'Why did they build a wall up on top of the mountains?' asked Emma.

'To keep livestock away from the watercourses when they were building Silent Valley Reservoir,' answered Dad, indicating the huge water reservoir at the base of a nearby valley, where they had parked the car and to which they were going to descend for their picnic lunch.

'So what's the question, Mr Kennedy?' asked Sammy.

'How long is the wall?

'Ah, Dad, how would we know that?!' said Maeve, laughing.

'Look at all the surrounding hills, calculate, and whoever is nearest gets the chocolate.'

'OK, let's try to figure it out,' said Dylan.

'You'll never figure it out!' retorted his sister. 'Just guess. Eh, I'll say ten miles, Mr Kennedy.'

'OK, Emma, ten miles. Anyone else?'

'I think it's more,' said Sammy. 'I'd say fifteen.'

'Maeve?'

'I'll split the difference. Twelve and a half.'

'I think it's way more,' said Dylan. 'I'm going to say twenty.'

'So who's right, Dad?' asked Maeve.

Her father pretended to open an envelope, like they did on television at the Oscars ceremony. 'And the winner of the 1969 Whit Monday Quiz is … Dylan Goldman!'

'Yes!' cried Dylan.

'It's actually twenty-two miles long. You were very close, Dylan, here's your prize.'

Maeve watched as her father gave Dylan a bar of chocolate.

'Thanks, Mr Kennedy.' he said, then quickly stuck his tongue out at Emma.

Before Emma could respond, Maeve saw her father grinning, and he addressed the others. 'And for each of the runners up – also a bar of chocolate!'

'Yes!' they cried.

Everyone took the chocolate, and Maeve laughed as Emma returned the gesture and stuck her tongue out at her brother. Maeve bit into the warm, slightly melted chocolate and she felt at peace with the world. Admittedly they were only about thirty miles from Belfast, and with each passing day the city seemed to be moving faster towards unrest. Even at home all wasn't well, and a couple of nights previously Maeve had overheard Dad offering to help out with extra money if Uncle Jim lost his job, which now seemed likely, despite his earlier reassurances to Maeve. But these were worries for another time, and right now she was having fun with her father and her friends. They hoisted their rucksacks onto their shoulders and began descending towards the reservoir, and she resolved to enjoy every minute of what was turning out to be a great day.

Sammy hated the smell of hospitals. Few things frightened him, but he associated the hospital smell with when his granny had been dying in Belfast's City Hospital, and the combined scent of disinfectant and polish made him feel queasy and a bit scared. But despite having argued against it with Maeve's father, he was now sitting in the X-ray department of that same hospital.

Looking back, Sammy had known he was in trouble the moment his ankle twisted. They had almost been back down on the valley floor beside the reservoir when he had lost his footing and gone over sharply on his left ankle. Immediately it had become too painful for him to put any weight on it. Maeve's Dad had trained in first aid in the army, and after carrying Sammy the short distance down to the road, Mr Kennedy had bound the ankle to stop it swelling up, then got Sammy to lie down with his leg raised and supported by a boulder, while he went to get the car.

Sammy felt bad about spoiling Maeve's big day out and he had tried to play down how painful the injury was. There was no fooling Mr Kennedy, however, and after examining the ankle in more detail, he had insisted it had to be x-rayed to make sure no bones were broken.

The journey back to Belfast had been muted, with Mr Kennedy driving carefully so as not to jolt the car, and Sammy trying not to show his pain whenever they hit a bump or pothole. Maeve, Dylan and Emma had been sympathetic, and in her usual optimistic way Maeve had bet that nothing was broken and that he was suffering from a bad sprain. As he waited now to be called in for the X-ray Sammy hoped fervently that she was right. But even if she was, there was still the big problem of what he would tell his father.

When Maeve had invited him on the daytrip he had eagerly accepted, but he had told Da that the trip was with Dylan and his family. What would Da say when he discovered that was a lie? And that Sammy had a secret friend who was a nationalist? He had thought of asking Mr Kennedy not to bring him home. But he could hardly say to Maeve's father: 'Thanks for looking after me, but don't bring me home. It's a problem that you're a Catholic.'

His mind was running in circles as he tried desperately to think of a way out. He had to find a way, because Da would kill him for telling a lie. And he would really go mad if he found out the Kennedys were nationalists, and that Mr Kennedy was in the Irish army. His reverie was suddenly cut short as a nurse approached with a chart. 'Sammy Taylor?' she said.

'Yes.'

'Right, Sammy, let's get you X-rayed.'

'Thanks,' he answered, anxious to get the procedure over with and to know if his ankle would be all right. Sammy rose to follow the nurse on his hospital crutches, and Maeve's father winked at him, while his friends wished him good luck. He nodded in reply and tried for a smile, but his stomach was in a knot as he wondered, yet again, what he would tell his father.

'Thanks for everything, Mr Kennedy' said Dylan as he stepped out of the car, just around the corner from Sammy's house.

'I'm not sure about this, Dylan,' said Maeve's father from behind the driver's wheel.

'Please, Mr Kennedy. Let me talk to Sammy's dad, it's definitely the best way,' said Dylan as persuasively as he could.

They were parked on Broadway, near enough to Sammy's house for him to walk there on the crutches, but not in direct view, lest Sammy's father might look out the window. The good news was that Sammy's ankle wasn't broken, just badly sprained. But although Sammy had been enormously relieved when the doctor had discharged him, he had confided to Dylan that he would be in big trouble when his da discovered that he hadn't spent the day with the Goldmans, but with Maeve and her father.

Dylan had realised at once that with a father so prejudiced and unstable, Sammy could easily end up getting a beating. After Sammy's loyalty in confronting Gordon Elliot, Dylan couldn't leave his friend to his fate, so he had done what Sammy couldn't do himself, and had discreetly explained the situation to Mr Kennedy. For once, being Jewish had been an advantage, and Dylan had pointed out to Maeve's father that the whole Catholic/Protestant issue wouldn't arise if it emerged that Sammy hurt his ankle while out with a Jewish friend.

Back at the hospital Mr Kennedy had very reluctantly gone along with Dylan's reasoning, but now that the moment had come he looked dubious,

'Please, Mr Kennedy,' said Dylan. 'If you just drop Sammy here I'll bring him in.'

Maeve's father still looked uneasy.

'Sammy's suffered enough today,' said Dylan, 'none of us want to see him in more trouble.'

Mr Kennedy hesitated, then breathed out. 'All right then,' he said. 'And mind that ankle, Sammy. Keep it raised as much as you can.'

'Thanks, Mr Kennedy, I will. And thanks for a great day out. Sorry I spoiled it.'

'Don't worry about that, son. Just mind yourself.'

'Good luck, Sammy,' said Maeve, and Emma gave him a thumbs up sign.

Dylan picked up Sammy's rucksack as well as his own, then tapped the roof of the car in farewell as Mr Kennedy started the engine.

'OK, Sammy,' said Dylan, his heart starting to pound at the thought of facing his friend's father, 'let's do it.'

Sammy nodded and gripped his crutches, then the two boys started for the house.

☣ ☣ ☣

'Damn it all, will I ever get some peace?! Why can't you be careful, and not land me with doctors and hospitals and God knows what?!'

'It wasn't Sammy's fault, Mr Taylor,' said Dylan. 'If anyone's to blame it's me.'

'And how's that?' asked Sammy's father aggressively.

They were in the living room in Ebor Street, the setting sun casting a mellow golden glow through the window. But there was nothing mellow about Mr Taylor, who had sent Sammy's sisters out of the room, in what Dylan felt was a worrying move.

'Please, Bill,' said Sammy's mother now, 'you don't have to bite off Dylan's nose.'

'Maybe I do! He's just said it was his fault.'

Dylan realised that Sammy was about to speak up, and he needed to get in first before his friend got into more trouble. Mr Taylor was frightening, with his red face and staring eyes, but

Dylan recalled how Sammy had been willing to fight Gordon with him, and he knew he had to be brave.

'I don't blame you for being angry with me,' he said. 'I shouldn't have gotten Sammy to race down the hill,' he added inventively, 'it was my fault, not his.'

Lying with a fluency that surprised himself, Dylan had explained that his own father had been called to the office in an emergency, causing the picnic to be cancelled, but that he had persuaded Sammy to take the train to the seaside at Bangor, where Sammy had sustained the injury.

Mr Taylor had asked how Sammy had travelled from the train to the hospital, and from the hospital to Ebor Street, and Dylan had explained that he had used his pocket money for taxis. It was one of the advantages of being viewed as a rich American that nobody had questioned this.

Mr Taylor drew nearer to Dylan now and glared at him. 'If you were my son I'd give you what for!' he growled.

'Bill,' said Mrs Taylor.

'I'm not talking to you, Rose, I'm talking to this fella,' he snapped. He turned back to Dylan. 'Aye, a proper hiding I'd give you!'

Dylan felt that this was bully behaviour, and before he knew what he was doing he said, 'It's well I'm not your son then.'

He saw the flash of anger in Mr Taylor's eyes. 'Maybe your own father needs to do it then. Maybe I'll have a chat with him.'

'I've already admitted it to him,' said Dylan, 'and I'll be punished. But my father doesn't beat me.'

He hadn't told Dad, but now he would have to explain the circumstances and hope his father would approve of his acting to protect Sammy.

Mr Taylor seemed briefly taken aback, and to Dylan's relief Sammy's mother spoke up.

'Well, I think the best thing is for Sammy to get himself off to bed now. Thank you, Dylan, for getting him safely back to us.'

Dylan had been offered an exit line, and now that Sammy would be safely in bed he decided to move quickly. 'See you, Sammy. Hope your ankle is better in the morning.'

'Thanks, Dylan. See you.'

'Goodnight, Mrs Taylor, Mr Taylor.'

Sammy's father didn't respond, but his mother gave him a quick conspiratorial wink. 'Good night, Dylan,' she said.

Dylan nodded briefly in acknowledgement, then he crossed to the hall door, stepped out onto Ebor Street and breathed an enormous sigh of relief.

CHAPTER SIXTEEN

'**M**en on the moon, what will they think of next?!' said Mr Doyle as he walked back along the running track with Emma and Maeve after training.

'Well, they haven't actually landed yet,' said Emma.

'Sure they're taking off next month. I saw it on the goggle box,' answered Mr Doyle.

Emma glanced at Maeve and grinned. Only someone as old-fashioned as Mr Doyle could refer to television as "the goggle box".

'Travelling from Florida to the moon!' The trainer's Belfast accent became stronger when he was animated, and he looked at Emma in the dusk of the summer evening, his eyes slightly bulging. 'The moon! When I was young, going to the sea in Bangor was an expedition.'

'Well, the moon is a bit further than Bangor,' admitted Emma with a smile. She found Mr Doyle entertaining, they had just had a satisfying training session, and life was good right now.

It was eleven days since Sammy had injured his ankle, and to everyone's relief he had made a fast recovery. Dylan had told their father the whole story, and Emma hadn't been too surprised when Dad agreed, with a little persuasion, to back up Dylan's story to Mr Taylor. Normally Dad insisted on truthfulness, but he knew first-hand how unreasonable Sammy's father could be, and he had gone along with Dylan's tale to protect Sammy. The one negative thing was that three days ago Maeve's father had gone back to the army in Cyprus, and Emma could see that tonight Maeve was a bit subdued. Emma's thoughts were interrupted when Mr Doyle suddenly stopped in his tracks.

'Mother of God, look at that young fella!' he said, indicating a boy who was walking along the top of the boundary wall on the far side of the running track. 'Get down off that wall, you wee pup, ye!' shouted Mr Doyle, moving away from the girls at speed, and making for the offending boy.

'You wee pup, ye!' said Emma, accurately mimicking the trainer.

Maeve smiled, and Emma continued enthusiastically. 'We have to use Mr D for our documentary, Maeve, he'd be brilliant.'

After much discussion, Emma and Maeve had agreed to make their documentary on the subject of accents. What with Mom's American accent, Dad's English one, her own and Dylan's originally English but now American accents, and Maeve's Belfast accent with an underlay of Dublin, they already had a range of voices to explore.

'Yeah, I suppose we could ask him,' answered Maeve.

Emma could see that her friend lacked her usual sparkle and she put her hand on her arm.

'I know it's tough,' she said gently.

'What is?'

'With your dad gone back. I know you really enjoyed having him here. He was lovely, so I understand how–'

Maeve's eyes welled up with tears, and Emma stopped mid sentence. She squeezed her friend's arm. 'Sorry, Maeve, I didn't mean …'

'It's OK.'

But Emma could see that it wasn't OK, and that tears were rolling down Maeve's cheeks.

'Let's sit down over there,' she said, guiding her friend to a seat around the corner from the changing room. They sat down together on the creaky wooden bench, and Emma put her arm around Maeve as the other girl dabbed at her eyes.

'I just wish … I just wish he hadn't to go back,' said Maeve.

'Sure.'

'It's like … it's like people are always leaving me. First Mam, and now Dad…'

The tears were rolling freely, and Maeve snuffled, then tried to dry her eyes again.

'I'm sorry, Emma. I'm sorry for being …'

'It's fine,' said Emma soothingly as she stroked her friend's hair. 'It's OK to cry, Maeve, better to let it out.'

After a moment Maeve gathered herself and looked at Emma with tearstained eyes.

'Don't get me wrong. Aunt Nan and Uncle Jim are great. But it's not the same as your own father. And I've been remembering things from when Mam was alive and the three of us were together.'

Maeve rarely spoke of her dead mother, and Emma asked softly. 'What was she like?'

'She was really funny. She could always make me laugh.'

'That must be where you got your sense of humour.'

'Maybe,' answered Maeve, trying for a wan smile. 'Though I didn't laugh for long time after she died.'

'Of course not.'

'And having Dad here for two weeks was brilliant, just brilliant. But then when he left…'

'I know.'

Maeve composed herself a little and spoke more strongly. 'Don't mind me, Emma, I'm just feeling a bit sorry for myself. I'll be fine.'

Emma squeezed her shoulder. 'Of course you will. But till you are, friends are there to help each other, right?'

'Right.'

'So if you feel down and want to talk, tell me. You don't have to pretend you're OK, not with me. Is that a deal?'

'That's a deal. And Emma?

'Yeah?'

'Thanks You're … you're the best friend I ever had.'

Now it was Emma's turn to feel tearful. 'Thanks, Maeve', she said softly. She quickly wiped her own eyes and smiled ruefully. 'What are we like?'

'I don't know. But I feel better. Will we head back before Mr D finds us?'

'OK,' answered Emma.

They stood up, and Emma felt deeply touched by the compliment that Maeve had just paid her. Then the two friends made for the changing room, walking arm in arm in the dark blue of the summer dusk.

'Her and her exhibition!' said Sammy's father. 'As if we'd go to that!'

Sammy was in the kitchen with his parents, and an invitation to Mrs Goldman's art exhibition had come in the post.

'I think it was nice of her to ask us,' said Sammy's mother.

'Nice of her?!' Da snorted. 'And her young fella after nearly wrecking our Sammy's ankle!'

It was three weeks now since Sammy had twisted his ankle and he wished Da would let the matter drop. 'I'm back training and all, Da,' he said reasonably. 'My ankle is fine.'

'It mightn't have been! It could easily have been broken. And she thinks she can act like nothing's happened and ask us to her "art exhibition".'

'In fairness, Bill, Dylan was very apologetic about the accident,' said Ma.

'That was big of him.'

'Sammy is grand, it all worked out OK.'

'I still don't know what they're at, inviting us to something like that.'

'We've had dealings with Mr Goldman, they're just being friendly.'

Sammy was tempted to say that the Goldmans were simply generous and inviting by nature, but he said nothing, not wanting to annoy his father.

'Our dealings are business,' said Da. 'Goldman is always going on about that. So why pretend that someone you do business with is your friend?'

'It's probably because Sammy and Dylan are friends,' suggested Ma. 'Anyway I think it would be interesting to go.'

Da looked at her in disbelief. 'You're not serious.'

'Come on, Bill, it would be something different.'

'Put it out of your head, we're not going to be made laughing stocks of.'

'How would we be laughing stocks?' asked Ma.

'Talking rubbish with a crowd of arty types? We'd look well!' said Da with a bitter laugh.

Sammy rarely sided with his father against Ma, but a part of him thought Da had a point, and that they might be uncomfortably out of their depth at the art exhibition.

'We don't have to pretend to be anything we're not,' said Ma. 'But I've never been to anything like this. It might be really nice.'

'Is there something wrong with your hearing, woman?! I'm not going, so forget it.'

'All right then,' said Ma, 'you don't have to. But I'm going.'

Sammy was really surprised. Normally Ma pleased his father to keep the peace. Occasionally, though, she made a stand – he just hadn't expected it to be over an art exhibition.

'Don't be ridiculous!' said Da.

'I'm not being ridiculous.'

'Of course you are!'

'What's ridiculous about accepting an invitation?'

'To go without your husband to something where you'll know nobody?'

'I'll know Dylan, and Mr Goldman, and Sammy.'

Sammy had been asked by Dylan's mother to help out at the exhibition, but he had never expected that his own mother would be on the guest list. He could see that Da was angry, but his mother had a determined look on her face and she didn't flinch when Da drew nearer to her.

'Are you trying to defy me?' he asked.

'No. But you won't come. And I've a right to go out if I want.'

'Oh, you've a right, have you?! It's not enough to listen to the Taigs, we're going to have civil rights at home too!'

'I'm not arguing with you, Bill,' said Ma calmly. 'But I'm accepting the invitation.' Before Da could say anything else, Ma turned on her heel and went up the stairs.

'See you later, Da,' said Sammy.

He made for the door, knowing that it would be a good idea to get out of Da's way right now. Sammy opened the hall door and headed down Ebor Street where a game of soccer was in progress. It was just what he needed to calm his buzzing head, he thought. On the one hand he was delighted that Ma had won a battle and stood up to Da. But Ma was a factory worker, and there wouldn't be many other people at the exhibition who worked in a mill. Would she stick out like a sore thumb and be really sorry that she had gone? Sammy didn't know, and as he reached the boys playing football at the corner of Kilburn Street he hoped she would be OK, then put his worries aside, greeted the other boys and joined in the game.

CHAPTER SEVENTEEN

'I have a question,' said Emma.

'This is going to be silly, I can tell,' cut in Dylan.

'Don't be such a spoilsport,' Emma told her brother, and Maeve smiled, enjoying the banter between the twins as the group of friends relaxed in the Goldmans' back garden.

'What's the question?' asked Sammy.

'How did Noah see the ark at night?'

'Please say you didn't get this from Mom's joke book,' said Dylan.

'Don't mind him, Emma,' said Maeve with a smile. 'How did Noah see the ark at night?'

'Flood lights!'

'Aw please!' protested Dylan, but even as he said it he was smiling.

'I think that's pretty good, actually,' said Sammy.

Maeve laughed happily at her friend's joke. She still missed her father, but it was several weeks now since he had gone back to Cyprus, and she had taken Emma's advice and carried on as best she could.

Today they were having a mini barbecue to celebrate the last day of the school year, and Dylan had cooked delicious hamburgers and sausages over the hot coals, the mild evening air scented with a whiff of charcoal and the mouth-watering smell of grilled meat. Maeve had brought along coconut cakes baked by Aunt Nan – she knew that Sammy loved coconut – and Mrs Goldman had provided them with chilled bottles of Coca Cola and lemonade.

Much as Maeve had enjoyed the big adult barbecues that the Goldmans threw, somehow this was better for being their own private celebration. She looked fondly at Emma, as her friend poured out more drinks for her guests. If she hadn't met the other girl she would never have been exposed to this world, and wouldn't have become friends with a boy like Sammy, whom she really liked now, despite their families being from communities that were increasingly at odds.

Dylan bit into his hamburger, then chewed as though in ecstasy. 'Hmm, wonderfully cooked. My compliments to the chef!' he said in a silly voice. He sipped his cola and nodded appreciatively. 'And Coca Cola nineteen sixty-nine, an excellent year!'

Maeve laughed. 'We should record that voice as one of our accents, Emma,' she said.

'Yeah, how is your documentary coming along?' asked Sammy.

'Pretty good,' answered Emma. 'We've recorded Mom and Dad, and some pupils in my school.'

'And I've recorded Uncle Jim and Aunt Nan. Uncle Jim is from Belfast, but Aunt Nan only came here after she got married, so they've different accents.'

'And what are you trying to do?' asked Sammy, 'Explain where accents come from?'

'Sort of,' answered Emma. 'Like why is it that some of the kids at the tennis club are from Belfast, but they don't have real Belfast accents?'

'That's because they're too posh,' said Sammy. 'But if you want proper Belfast accents you should record on my street.'

'Great, let's do that then,' said Emma enthusiastically.

Maeve was struck again by how open to other people the Goldmans were. As far as Maeve could see, most rich people were friends with other rich people, and those who were working class made friends in their own class. But Emma had said that her father wanted the family to meet people from all backgrounds, in whatever place his work took him. It explained why Emma went for private ballet lessons and was a member of a fancy tennis club, yet also ran with Ardara Harriers and was friends with someone like herself, a girl from the working class Falls Road area.

'Brilliant coconut cakes, Maeve,' said Sammy, after biting into one of her aunt's buns.

'Aunt Nan's secret recipe. She'll pass it on to me on her deathbed!'

Sammy grinned, then looked thoughtful. 'You know, if you're going to come down to Ebor Street to record, you should come on a parade day. You'd get loads of different people then.'

'When is the next parade?' asked Dylan.

'In about a week. We always have a big one at the start of July.'

'And they wouldn't mind us recording them?' asked Emma.

'No, sure you'd be with me.'

'Great.'

Maeve could see that Emma was enthusiastic, but she had been taken aback by Sammy's comment. She looked at him now and put a question that she felt she had to ask. 'When you say we've a big parade, Sammy, do you mean that you march?'

'Well, we cheer them on. But it's adults in the Orange Lodges who parade.'

'Why?'

Sammy looked slightly confused. 'Why what?'

'Why do they parade?'

'Sure they've always paraded.'

'Yes, but that's just saying what they do. But why parade?'

Sammy hesitated. 'It's just … it's to mark the Somme, or The Twelfth.'

'What are they?' asked Emma.

'The twelfth of July is the date of the Battle of the Boyne; the first of July is the Battle of the Somme. They're big days for Orangemen, so they march to celebrate them.'

'Do they not really march to annoy Catholics?' asked Maeve. 'To show them who's boss? That they'll march along their streets whether they like it or not?'

Sammy looked uncomfortable. Maeve sensed that he hadn't thought this out fully, but that he was too honest to deny that there was truth in what she said.

'A lot of it … a lot of it is fun,' said Sammy. 'Like, there're bonfires, and street parties, and bands and drumming and all that.'

'I'm sure there is. And I'm not looking to fight with you, Sammy,' said Maeve. 'But it's not much fun for people who feel surrounded, with Lambeg drums being pounded outside their doors, outside their churches, in areas where the Orangemen don't live.'

Sammy looked thoughtful, but before he could reply, Dylan spoke up. 'What happened our rule, folks?'

'Yeah,' said Emma. 'We said when we were together we weren't Jews, or Catholics or Protestants – just friends. That we'd leave all that stuff outside?'

Maeve looked at the twins and realised that they were right. 'Sorry,' she said. 'I didn't mean to break the rule. The parade thing just came up, but I don't want us to fall out.' She turned to Sammy, hoping that she hadn't spoiled things. 'Friends?' she asked.

There was a brief pause while Sammy looked back at her seriously. Then he spoke 'How could we not be, when your aunt makes brilliant coconut cakes?' He grinned, then offered his hand.

Maeve smiled in return. She thought that shaking hands was a bit formal, but she was relieved that the tension was eased and shook Sammy's hand.

'Right,' said Emma happily. 'Now that's sorted out, let's make ourselves sick eating hamburgers and coconut cake. All in favour say "aye"!'

'Aye!' they all cried.

Mom was in her element. She had gone into full hippy mode for tonight's exhibition, and Emma smiled as she watched her mother greeting the guests, dressed in a kaftan, and with her hair held back by a spangled headband. Dad was wearing a wine-coloured velvet jacket, and although some grey had appeared in his thick blond hair he wore it fairly long and looked suitably fashionable. But although Dad could fit in with tonight's arty crowd, he still had a practical side and had convinced Mom that placing joss sticks around the gallery was a step too far. Mom had given way on that one, but had insisted on Eastern music being played through the speakers, and the sitar playing of Ravi Shankar could be heard now, giving the occasion an air of cool trendiness.

In contrast to Mom's hippy look, Sammy's mother, Mrs Taylor, was wearing a conservative floral dress, which Emma suspected was probably her best outfit. Emma had thought that Mrs Taylor looked a bit lost in the aftermath of being introduced to Mom, who then got pulled away to meet an art critic. Feeling a little sorry for her, Emma had chatted to Sammy's mother, and had been slightly surprised to find how interesting she was. Emma had often seen the huge mill buildings that were such a feature of Belfast, but she had never been inside one, and Mrs Taylor had just told her about the history of Belfast's linen industry, and what it was like to work in one of the city's biggest mills.

'It sounds like the stuff you make is beautiful,' said Emma, 'but it also sounds like really hard work.'

'It's all of that,' said Mrs Taylor with a wry smile.

'So, would you prefer to do something else?'

'I'm not qualified for anything else, love. And even though the pay's not great, it's still a job. And there's plenty would take your place if you don't hold onto it.'

'Right,' said Emma. She knew Sammy's family wasn't well off, but it was only when Mrs Taylor had told her about conditions in the mills that she realised how gruelling life was for many people.

'Now – reinforcements!' said Dylan, as he and Sammy suddenly arrived with the plates of hors d'oeuvres that they were serving to the guests. 'More cheese, Mrs Taylor?'

'Thank you, Dylan, I don't mind if I do.'

'Another olive, Ma?' said Sammy, offering his plate.

Mrs Taylor looked at Emma and smiled. 'I've never had olives before, but they're delicious! Thanks, Sammy,' she said, taking an olive that was skewered on a little wooden stick.

'I can't wait to see Da's face when we start having olives at home!' said Sammy with a grin.

'Sammy's da would be a wee bit set in his ways,' explained Mrs Taylor, 'when it comes to food.'

Or anything else, thought Emma, though of course she didn't say it. She wondered what Mr Taylor would think of Mom's gesture to feminism, whereby she had inverted the usual custom of girls helping to serve food, and instead asked Dylan and Sammy to circulate with the plates of hors d'oeuvres. Before she could think about it any more she caught sight of Maeve and her aunt, and she turned to Sammy's mother.

'Mrs Taylor, can I introduce you to my friend Maeve, and her aunt?'

'Yes, I'd love to meet them.'

'Carry on, boys, guests to be fed!' said Emma playfully.

Sammy pretended to throw the plate of olives at her, and Dylan contented himself with making a face, then Emma led Mrs Taylor across the room.

'Hi, Maeve. Hi, Mrs Sweeney. I'd like you to meet Sammy's mother, Mrs Taylor.'

Maeve and her aunt shook hands, and Emma watched carefully to see how the two women responded to one another. Shortly after arriving in Belfast, Emma had been shocked to be told that the first thing people in Northern Ireland did on being introduced was to figure out to which of the two tribes the other person belonged. With a name like Taylor, Sammy's mother was probably Protestant, while Maeve's Aunt Nan, with a name like Sweeney, was probably Catholic. But if the two women were sizing each other up Emma wasn't aware of it, and the mood between them seemed relaxed and friendly. Maeve's aunt explained that her husband had lost his job and couldn't be here tonight as he was in Donegal, meeting a builder who might have another job for him. Mrs Taylor sympathised over the job loss and said that her own husband had to visit a sick relation tonight.

Emma looked at Maeve and raised her eyebrow. They both knew what Sammy's father was like and that this was almost certainly a polite lie.

'Your mother is very talented, Emma,' said Maeve's aunt now.

'Thanks, Mrs Sweeney, I'll tell her you said that!'

'We've already told her,' explained Maeve.

'Yeah? Don't give her a swelled head, I have to live with her,' replied Emma with a smile.

'I wasn't sure what to expect,' said Sammy's mother. 'I don't know anything about art, and some of the stuff they call art nowadays ...' she opened her hands in a gesture of despair, before smiling. 'But your mother's landscapes are wonderful.'

Emma thought she looked like Sammy when she smiled, and she was touched by the woman's sincerity. 'Thanks, Mrs Taylor.'

'How long will the exhibition run?' asked Maeve's aunt.

'About a month,' answered Emma. 'We're going off on holidays for three weeks on Monday, but the gallery will let Mom know how sales are going.'

'I'm sure they'll sell very well,' said Sammy's mother. 'And where are you off to?'

'Nerja, in Spain. Dad's promised us a break for ages, and Mom is exhausted after all the work for the exhibition. So, three weeks in the Spanish sun ...'

'Sounds brilliant,' said Maeve, 'but we'll really miss you and Dylan.'

'We'll miss you too. But you'll have Sammy to keep you company.' As soon as she said it Emma wondered if this was a mistake. While the Sweeneys and the Taylors each knew that Maeve and Sammy had become friend with the Goldmans, she wasn't sure how much they knew about Sammy and Maeve also being friends.

Before she could consider it any further they were all distracted by the sound of smashing glass in the street outside. Emma knew from Dad about the protest marches and riots that were convulsing Northern Ireland. Now, first hand, she saw Royal Ulster Constabulary Land Rovers screeching to a halt across the street below the window of the gallery. Bricks and other missiles began to rain down on the RUC men, and Emma felt her stomach tighten in fear as she realised that a riot was erupting right below her.

'Get back from the windows!' cried her father, crossing the room toward her. 'Get back from the windows, everybody!'

Emma quickly stepped back from the gallery windows. She had no idea how the riot had started and was frightened at how suddenly the violence had erupted. She could hear screaming and shouting, and the sound of police sirens approaching. Without warning, a window further down the room was shattered, and a brick skidded across the floor of the gallery. Several of the guests screamed in shock, and Emma swallowed hard. For weeks people had been saying that Northern Ireland was on the brink of sectarian warfare, and now, suddenly, terrifyingly, Emma realised that they were right, and that chaos was coming.

PART THREE

BOILING POINT

CHAPTER EIGHTEEN

Fighting and rioting seemed light years away as Dylan lay on a lounger by the hotel swimming pool, savouring the hot sun that shone in a clear blue sky. The scent of jasmine hung in the air, and his favourite pop song of the moment, 'I Heard It Through the Grapevine' was playing from the poolside speakers. He could see his mother tapping out the rhythm of the song with her fingers as she lay back on her lounger, while Emma sat beside him engrossed in her book. They were a week into their stay in Nerja, and Dylan almost felt guilty at how much he was enjoying the family's Spanish holiday, knowing that Northern Ireland was in turmoil.

After the major Orange marches on the twelfth of July there had been widespread rioting, with serious violence in Derry, Dungiven and Belfast. In some districts families had had to flee their homes, and Dylan hoped that Sammy and Maeve would be safe amidst all the trouble. He had brought postcards down to the pool, but now he feared that sending a postcard enthusing about Nerja might seem insensitive when his friends were in the middle of so much conflict. On the other hand he had promised to write, and he didn't want them to think he was being rude or had forgotten about them. He sat up on his lounger and turned to Emma.

'Do you think I should still send postcards to Sammy and Maeve?'

Emma lowered her book and looked at him. 'Why wouldn't you?'

'There's so much trouble in Belfast, but we're having a great time. I don't want it to sound like I'm rubbing it in.'

'Maeve and Sammy know you better than that. We said we'd send them cards, so we should.'

'Yeah, you're probably right,' said Dylan. 'I just hope they're OK.'

'They'll stay out of trouble.' Emma put her book down, then spoke softly so that her mother wouldn't hear. 'Will they be able to stay friends, though?'

'Of course.'

'There's no *of course*, Dylan. With Protestants and Catholics attacking each other, they mightn't be allowed.'

'I don't think they've said much at home about being friends with one another.'

'But Mrs Taylor and Aunt Nan saw we were all friends the night of Mom's exhibition.'

'Yes, but I'd say Mrs Taylor thinks Sammy is friends with me, and Maeve's aunt probably thinks the same about you and Maeve.'

'Maybe,' said Emma, 'but it's really mad that we couldn't all just be friends openly.'

'The whole thing is really mad,' answered Dylan, then he noticed his father approaching. Dad had gone into the hotel to make some phone calls, and Dylan saw that his face looked grim. 'Everything OK, Dad?' he asked.

'No, I'm afraid not.'

Mom sat up on her lounger. 'What's wrong?'

Dylan watched carefully as his father answered. 'I was on to Belfast. It was only a matter of time till someone was killed. Now a man who was batoned by the police has died.'

'Oh no,' said Mom. 'That's awful.'

'Yeah. And I know you don't want to hear this, but I should be back there, covering it.'

'You're entitled to a holiday, David,' said Mom. 'We all are.'

'Not while a country unravels. It's my job, Julie; I need to be covering it.'

Mom seemed like she was going to respond, but Dad looked her in the eye.

'You know I do,' he said.

Mom said nothing, and Dylan sensed that this was her way of reluctantly agreeing.

Emma, however, spoke up. 'Does that mean we have to cut short our holiday?'

Dylan was enjoying Spain, and hoped his father wouldn't end their time in Nerja.

'This is turning into a major story,' answered Dad. 'I have to be back there on the ground. But there's no reason for the rest of you to end your holiday.'

Dylan felt selfish now for wanting to stay on, and worried too that his father might get caught up in the vicious rioting. As if reading his thoughts, Emma spoke up again.

'But if you go back, Dad, it could be dangerous. You could get hurt.'

'No, love. It's dangerous for the people involved in the trouble, no question. But journalists like me aren't involved with either side, we're simply reporting.'

'But even so, Dad–' began Dylan, before being cut short by his father swiftly raising his hand.

'No "buts",' said Dad. 'Your mom is right, you all deserve a holiday. So you stay on and enjoy it, I won't hear of anyone else coming back – that's final. And we'll all get away together for Rosh Hashanah, I promise.'

Rosh Hashanah was the Jewish New Year, and Dylan always enjoyed their annual visit to Leeds to celebrate it with his grandparents. He couldn't get excited about it now, however.

'Don't worry, I'll ring every day to let you know I'm fine,' said Dad. 'OK?'

Emma reluctantly nodded in agreement.

'Dylan?'

'Yeah, OK, Dad,' he answered. But even as he said it he realised that the holiday wouldn't be the same now. And despite Dad's assurances, he would worry about his father, and his friends, and the trouble that was spreading across Belfast.

'Men on the moon, me backside!' said Da, as he cast his fishing line out over the gently-flowing waters of the river Lagan. 'Won't put bread on our table, will it?'

'I suppose not, Da,' said Sammy with a smile.

The first astronauts had landed on the moon, and half the world seemed to be going mad with excitement, but Sammy was amused by his father's practical view of how little it would affect their lives. He cast his own line out over the river, its surface rippled by a soft July breeze. It was at times like this that he got on best with Da, and he knew that his sisters begrudged him the treat of going fishing with their father.

'What's the point of going to the moon?' said Da. 'It must have cost millions of dollars – billions, probably. Take that money, divide it between every man, woman and child in America, and then everyone would have got something out of it. Amn't I right?'

'Yeah,' said Sammy.

'And as for your man's speech: *One small step for man, one giant leap for mankind*, I bet he thought that was really smart. I bet he spent weeks making that up!'

Even though Da was being negative, he was doing it in a good-humoured way that Sammy found entertaining.

'Moon landing, me eye!' said his father. 'Linfield for the cup and more fish in the Lagan, eh, Sammy?!'

'Now you're talking, Da!'

Sammy watched as his father settled back easily on the river bank, and he allowed his own thoughts to wander. The last ten days had seen widespread rioting, and things seemed to be getting worse by the day. Despite that, he had met up with Maeve, and they had grown friendlier while the Goldmans were away on holidays. Both Sammy and Maeve had summer jobs so they couldn't get together during the day, but on several evenings they had arranged to meet, and he had even gone into the forbidden territory of the Falls Road to cheer her on in a race, and to meet the famous Mr D, Maeve's colourful coach. The more he got to know her the more he liked her, and although he didn't share her nationalist views, he had found himself influenced by some of the things she said.

Sammy had always loved the bonfires and celebrations on the eve of the twefth of July, but though he had enjoyed the fun at his local bonfire, this year he was aware of what Maeve had said about marching. He still thought that Orangemen were entitled to have their traditional marches, but maybe Maeve had a point about not deliberately provoking their Catholic neighbours.

Sammy watched his father as he adjusted his fishing line and thought how angry Da would be if he knew what he was thinking. Da had marched on the Twefth and his response to the violence that followed the marches this year was to blame the nationalists. Sammy, however, could see that it wasn't a black and white issue, and it was worrying that Da was so blinkered. Two civilians had been killed in the last week, and with the violence spreading, Sammy feared that his father was becoming involved with local men that were in the Ulster Volunteer Force. The UVF was the loyalist version of the IRA, the illegal nationalist army, and Sammy wished Da wouldn't get caught up with these men.

Saying anything on the subject now risked spoiling the mood, but in spite of all Da's faults Sammy cared for him and couldn't just do nothing. Now was his chance and maybe if he came at the subject sideways he could discuss the UVF without making his father angry. He was nervous and didn't know how to start, so he decided to plunge in before he lost his nerve. 'Da, can I ask you something?'

'What's that, son?'

'All the riots and fighting … what's … what's going to happen?'

'It's going to get worse.'

'Really?' This wasn't what Sammy had hoped to hear. 'Why's that, Da?'

'Because the marching season is in full swing. The Taigs have lost the run of themselves with all this civil rights stuff. Telling us where we can march? Over my dead body! Or better yet, over their dead bodies!'

His father said this with a bitter laugh, but Sammy saw nothing remotely funny about it.

'If anything happened you, Da, it would be … it would be awful for the family.'

'I can handle myself, nothing will happen me.'

'Yes, but–'

'Relax, Sammy,' said Da authoratively. 'I know what I'm doing.'

There was no way to bring up the UVF now, so Sammy nodded. 'OK, Da.'

'It's the Taigs who need to worry,' continued his father.

'Yeah?'

'The Specials are mobilised. The police are getting stuck in. If the Taigs fancy their chances in an uprising let them try it, and we'll slaughter them!'

Sammy was horrified. But surely talk of an uprising had to be an exaggeration. 'An uprising, Da? Could that happen?'

'Some of our lads expect it. Even if there's not an actual uprising, you mark my words, things are coming to a head.' Just then Da got a bite on his line, and he began reeling in.

Sammy looked out across the peacefully flowing waters of the Lagan, but the peacefulness was misleading, and he felt that his father might be right, and that the worst was yet to come.

CHAPTER NINETEEN

'It was a brilliant book, I couldn't put it down!' said Maeve.

'I was the same,' agreed Sammy.

'Aunt Nan even caught me reading it in bed with a torch.'

'Did you get in trouble?'

'A bit. And I was bleary-eyed next morning, but I didn't care, I had to find out what happened after the kidnapping!'

Maeve and Sammy were sitting on the grass in Donegall Square, the ornate façade of Belfast City Hall framed behind them against the blue of the evening sky. The city centre location was a neutral venue, neither loyalist nor nationalist. Because it was about the same distance from both their homes, Maeve had arranged to meet there to return a novel that Sammy had lent her.

'It's the best adventure story I've read in ages,' she said.

'Yeah, it's kind of a boy's story, but I thought you might like it.'

Maeve wasn't sure this was a compliment and she looked at him quizzically.

'Why – because I'm a tomboy?'

'No,' answered Sammy at once. 'No, it's because … well, because you're adventurous yourself.'

This was a better answer, Maeve thought, but she wasn't going to let Sammy off completely. 'Besides,' she said, 'why shouldn't girls enjoy adventure stories as much as boys?'

Sammy thought a moment, then nodded. 'No reason really, I suppose.'

One of the things Maeve liked about Sammy was that he wasn't set in his ways, and if you made a good point he could be swayed by it. She smiled at him now. 'Anyway, thanks again for the lend.'

'You're grand.'

Maeve leaned back and looked up at the evening sky, where the first hints of dusk were darkening its colour. 'What would you say the twins are doing now?' she asked.

Sammy considered briefly. 'Emma's probably stopping Spanish people in the street to record their accents,' he answered with a grin. 'And Dylan is probably trying to dazzle the locals with his soccer skills!'

Maeve nodded. 'I'd say you're not a million miles off.'

'It'll be good to have them back, won't it?'

'Yeah, I'm dying to see them.'

The Goldmans had been gone for nearly three weeks now, but were due back in a couple of days. But although Maeve missed Emma and Dylan, she had become closer to Sammy while their mutual friends were away. They had become trusting enough to exchange confidences, and Maeve had felt flattered when Sammy revealed to her his secret dream of one day being a doctor. She in turn had told him of her wish that Da would leave the army, and that they would live together in Maeve's dream house – whose back garden would run down to a river!

Maeve was friends with other girls in her neighbourhood, but it was nice to have a friend like Sammy that you could share confidences with, and Maeve thought that her increased closeness with him was the one good thing to come out of a bad period of growing violence.

'So, are you nearly finished making the documentary?' asked Sammy now.

'Yeah. Emma has been showing me how to edit the tapes.'

'What does that mean?'

'It's where you take all the recordings and pick out the best bits. Then you can rearrange them and use music to put it all together as a programme. Mr Goldman taught Emma.'

'Sounds brilliant,' said Sammy, 'I'm dying to hear it. Well, apart from hearing my own voice.'

'Yeah, it's weird how different the recording is from how you think you sound!'

Just then a nearby clock tolled out the hour and Sammy stretched, before getting up. 'I'd better be heading back.'

'Me too,' agreed Maeve as she rose from the grass.

'See you on Tuesday night in Goldmans?' said Sammy, referring to a reunion that had been agreed even before the twins had set off for Spain.

'Definitely,' said Maeve. 'And Sammy?'

'Yeah?'

'Don't Lose your Hucklebuck Shoes!' This was the title of a pop song, and had become a jokey catchphrase between the four friends.

'Never go anywhere without them!' said Sammy, then he gave a wave of farewell and headed off in the direction of Donegall Road.

Maeve turned away and began walking along Wellington Place, making for Albert Street and the way back to her neighbourhood. She hadn't told her aunt and uncle that she was meeting Sammy, and now she speeded up her pace. She wanted to be home before the dusk deepened, and before the other children of the neighbourhood – with whom Aunt Nan would assume she was playing – were called in for the night. She reached the Lower Falls Road, then turned into Sevastopol Street and headed towards Clonard Gardens and the monastery. At the junction of Bombay Street she greeted some of the neighbourhood girls who were playing skipping, but she didn't linger and instead made for her hall door. She knew that some of the local kids resented her friendship with the Goldmans. One really spiteful girl, Cathy Riordan, had even said she was a Jew-lover. Maeve had told Cathy bluntly that she was pathetic, and she had resolved that she wasn't going to let other people decide who her friends were. Emma, Dylan and Sammy had turned out to be great friends, and she was pleased that while loyalists and nationalists had been at each other's throats recently, she and Sammy had become even firmer friends.

She opened the hall door and entered the house, to find Aunt Nan and Uncle Jim sitting at the kitchen table. She greeted them but picked up on a tense atmosphere. 'What's wrong?' asked Maeve.

'I've been offered a full time job, but it's in Donegal,' said her uncle.

Maeve realised at once what a dilemma this presented. Donegal was too far from Belfast for him to commute, so he would only see them at weekends. Maeve had overheard her aunt and uncle arguing during the week, with Uncle Jim insisting that he couldn't take any more charity from her father. Maeve actually thought there was no shame in family members helping each other out. Aunt Nan was a full time housewife who also did some voluntary work with the elderly, and Maeve felt that Uncle Jim put too much importance on being the sole provider. But that was his nature, and his pride was at stake, so now she tried to be supportive. 'Well, if that's where you have to go, Uncle Jim, that's where you have to go. It'll probably only be for a while.'

'That's what I've been saying,' said Aunt Nan.

'If it was any other time I wouldn't hesitate,' said her uncle. 'But with all this trouble I'm not happy leaving you alone here.'

'We'll be fine, Jim. Things will settle down eventually.'

Maeve wasn't so sure about that. And now that she had been forced to think about it, it would be a bit scary not having the comforting presence of her uncle about the place. But she had to be brave. 'It'll be all right, Uncle Jim, we'll manage OK.'

Maeve could see that he was nearly persuaded. 'Really we will. Aunt Nan and I will look out for each other, won't we, Aunt Nan?'

'Of course we will.'

Uncle Jim hesitated for a moment more, then nodded. 'All right then. I'll tell them I'm taking the job.'

'Great,' said Maeve, 'congratulations.' She smiled reassuringly at her uncle, and hoped that she had done the right thing.

'There's so much to catch up on,' said Emma, 'I don't know where to start!'

'Start by serving up the hamburgers,' said Dylan as he flipped the last one off the barbecue and onto a plate, 'we're all starving.'

Emma served up the food with a smile, delighted to be back with her friends. She had arrived in Belfast with Mom and Dylan the previous day, and it had been great to be reunited with Dad. She thought he looked tired from working so hard covering the conflict, but it had still been lovely to have all the family together again. And now, catching up with Maeve and Sammy, she complimented herself on having planned this reunion barbecue before she had left.

'So, what's been happening?' she asked as they relaxed in the back garden of her home, eating their food while a Beach Boys record played on her portable record player.

'Well, men landed on the moon while you were gone.' said Sammy between bites of his hamburger.

'I know that! They do have televisions in Spain.'

'And Tony Jacklin won the British Open in the golf,' added Sammy.

'Yeah, we heard about that too,' said Emma. 'But I meant what's been happening here.'

'Marches, riots, fighting,' said Maeve. 'But do we have to talk about that?

'Absolutely not,' said Dylan. 'We're still on holidays, so let's forget all that stuff. So, what have you two been up to?'

'Not much really,' answered Sammy. 'We went to Bangor on a family outing.'

'Sounds nice,' said Emma.

'Well, it was till my sister Florrie stuffed herself and vomited over Ma on the train home.'

'Thanks, Sammy,' said Emma, dramatically lowering her plate, 'I was actually enjoying my hamburger!'

'Sorry,' said Sammy with a grin. 'The other good thing was my da took me fishing. We caught trout and fried them for supper.'

'Brilliant,' said Dylan.

'What about you, Maeve?' asked Emma, returning to eating her burger.

'I went swimming at Donaghadee with my aunt and uncle, and we saw a sea lion.'

'Great. How is he, by the way?'

'The sea lion? He never said!'

Emma laughed. 'Your uncle. You said he'd lost his job.'

'He's getting a new one. But it means moving to Donegal, so we'll only see him at the weekends.'

'Pity we couldn't get my da a job in Donegal!' said Sammy.

He said it with a grin, but Emma couldn't help feeling that it would actually be good for Sammy and his family if their unpredictable father got a steady job that kept him over eighty miles distant. She couldn't say that, of course, so she switched the topic to holiday souvenirs. Pooling her money with Dylan, they had bought Sammy a leather belt and Maeve a Spanish shawl, and both friends had enthused about the presents. Now, though, she discussed her trainer. 'I never told you what I got for Mr D. I felt I had to get him some souvenir of Nerja, but he's really hard to buy for.'

'Buckie was easy,' said Dylan. 'I knew a bottle of Spanish brandy would be right up his alley!'

'But Mr D doesn't smoke or drink,' said Emma. 'And he wears really old fashioned clothes.'

Maeve grinned. 'No sombrero then?!'

'No. And apart from running, the only other thing we know he loves is the Irish language.'

'So what did you get him?' asked Maeve.

'A picture of the Madonna and Child,' answered Emma. 'He's dead religious, so we thought that might do it.'

'But then we were thinking,' said Dylan. 'He wouldn't feel there was anything wrong with Jews giving him a picture of Jesus, would he?'

'Gordon Elliott might think that, but I don't think anyone else would,' said Sammy.

'Mr D might even feel he was half way to converting you!' said Maeve with a laugh.

Emma felt relieved. She put down her empty plate. 'Apple pie anyone?'

'Sure why not?' answered Maeve. 'As Uncle Jim says, 'a refusal might give offence'!'

Emma laughed and began to cut the apple pie.

'Maeve told me you're nearly finished the documentary,' said Sammy.

'Yeah, we hope to get it wrapped up in the next couple of weeks. I'm really looking forward to finishing it.'

'And I'm really looking forward—' began Dylan, but he stopped mid-sentence.

A series of shots carried on the breeze from the direction of the city. For a moment nobody said anything, then Sammy spoke. 'It's getting worse.'

'Yeah,' said Maeve quietly. She held out her plate to Emma. 'That apple pie looks great,' she said.

Emma realised that her friend was gamely trying to keep the atmosphere going and to hold the outside world at bay. She smiled at Maeve and cut her a slice. But inside she had a sinking feeling that time was running out, and that nothing they could do would stop the trouble that was coming.

Buckie was trying to whip up the team with his pre-match talk, but today Dylan found it hard to concentrate on the coach's words. They were in the home dressing room for a match against a team from Woodvale, and instead of listening to Buckie, Dylan found his attention wandering to the coach's shining black eye.

Earlier he had given Buckie the present of the Spanish brandy. The coach had thanked him politely, but Dylan had sensed at once that the older man wasn't in the mood for banter, and he had resisted the temptation to ask about the injury. There had been serious rioting last weekend, and Dylan suspected that Buckie must have been involved as a part-time constable with the B Specials, or maybe simply as a loyalist rioter.

'OK, lads,' said the coach now, finishing up his talk. 'Go out there and get stuck in!' Buckie headed out towards the pitch, and Gordon Elliott smirked. 'I heard Buckie got stuck in himself. I wouldn't like to be the Taig who gave him that shiner!'

Some of the other boys laughed, but Dylan didn't join in. Since he and Sammy had confronted Gordon there had been no further trouble. Gordon was distant with him, but despite having been threatened by Sammy also, the two of them were now back on reasonable terms.

Sammy turned to the other boy with interest. 'Where was Buckie fighting?' he asked.

'Unity Flats,' answered Gordon. 'They came really close to driving the Taigs out of their den!'

The warren of Unity Flats was nationalist territory that bordered the fiercely loyalist Shankill Road. There had been pitched battles there over the weekend, and Dylan had heard from his father that at one stage the residents defending the flats had indeed almost been overrun. Dad had said that there could have been a bloodbath if that had happened, yet Gordon was treating the incident like it was a tight-run match that his team had almost won.

'Catholics have to live somewhere, Gordon,' said Sammy.

'They don't have to live on top of us! My da says the new flats should never have been given to Catholics; the Shankill's always been Protestant.'

'But the flats replaced old houses in Carrick Hill,' answered Dylan. 'And my father says that area was mainly Catholic.'

'Anyway the fighting's died down now,' interjected Sammy.

'Not for long,' said Gordon confidently 'The Apprentice Boys have a big march next weekend. If anyone tries to stop them marching through Londonderry there'll be all-out war.'

Dylan found Gordon's attitude depressing. But he had heard his father saying that the situation in Derry was like a powder keg waiting to go up, and he feared the other boy might be right. 'You sound like you can't wait for people to get hurt,' said Dylan.

Gordon looked unperturbed. 'If the Taigs want trouble we'll give it to them!'

'Supposing most people on both sides don't want trouble?'

'There's going to be trouble anyway!' said Gordon impatiently, then he pushed past Dylan and made for the dressing room door.

The rest of the players headed for the pitch, but Dylan stood there a moment, wondering how it would affect his family and friends if, as predicted, the powder keg was ignited next weekend.

PART FOUR

BREAKDOWN

CHAPTER TWENTY

Emma sat upright in bed. She had heard the sound of her father's car pulling into the drive and she glanced at the fluorescent hand of the clock. Two in the morning. She had been in bed for several hours but sleep was impossible. Northern Ireland had descended into chaos, with serious fighting between loyalists, nationalists and the police, in Derry, Belfast, Newry, Armagh and many other places. Here on the Malone Road she felt safe, but she was really worried about Maeve, whose home in Bombay Street was perilously close to where the nationalist Falls area met the ultra loyalist Shankill.

It seemed highly likely that there would be trouble there, and with Uncle Jim away in Donegal, Maeve and her aunt would be alone and vulnerable. Emma's father had been out all day covering the fighting and doing radio reports, and she quickly climbed out of bed, threw on her dressing gown and ran down the stairs, anxious to hear the latest news.

Her father was quietly closing the front door when Emma met him in the hall.

'Emma, what are you doing up?'

'I've been tossing and turning for ages.' She looked at her father and saw the exhaustion in his face. 'You look tired, Dad. Let me make you a cup of tea.'

'That would be good.'

Emma led the way into the kitchen and put on the kettle, while her father slumped down into his usual chair at the table.

'Have you had anything to eat, Dad?'

'Yeah, I got something earlier. Just the tea will be fine.'

Emma set out a cup and saucer and got milk from the fridge, then sat with her father as she waited for the kettle to boil. 'What's the latest, Dad?'

'It's awful. Two people were killed by machine-gun fire at Divis Street. One was just a child of nine.'

'Oh, no.'

'Mobs are burning people out of their homes. Things are really out of hand.'

After the recent Apprentice Boys march in Derry there had been a pitched battle between residents of the nationalist Bogside area and the police. The police had dispersed the Bogsiders, driving them back into their area, and had then tried to enter the area themselves. The battle had raged for over two days now and the Civil Rights Association had called for demonstrations elsewhere to help draw off police numbers from the Bogside. The call had been answered, but the result had been to ignite appalling violence right across Northern Ireland.

'So what's going to happen, Dad?'

'I don't know. The police are stretched too thin. It's getting out of control.'

'Yeah?'

'It's gone way beyond fist fights and stone throwing. It's rifles, machine guns, petrol bombs, shops and houses burnt to the ground.'

Emma felt sickened. 'Why do people want to do that?'

'Passions are high, and both sides assume the worst of each other.'

'But they both have to live here. Why can't they settle their differences without killing children and burning people's houses?'

Her father breathed out wearily. 'Good question, Emma. I suppose the answer is fear, really.'

'How do you mean?'

'The loyalists fear that this is an organised rebellion and that the nationalists are trying to overthrow the state.'

'And are they?'

'No. Some of them would like to, but it's not an insurrection. But loyalists I've talked to think it is. So they're frightened and they're enraged.'

'What about the nationalists?' asked Emma.

'They're afraid this is a religious pogrom. Catholics are out-numbered and surrounded here in Belfast. And they think the police are on the side of the Protestants. So they're barricading their streets and fighting the loyalists and the police.'

'Right.' Emma made tea and poured it for her father, who drank it gratefully.

'Dad, I'm … I'm really worried about Maeve.'

'Have you rung her?'

'They've no phone.'

'Sorry, Emma, you told me that before. It's been a long day, I'm not thinking straight.'

'Bombay Street is close to the Shankill Road, Dad. Were you up there?'

'I was in the general area.' Emma picked up on her father's unease.

'Is it bad?'

'It's bad in that whole area. I could only get so close.'

'I thought … I thought maybe Maeve could come and stay with us, just till things calm down a bit.'

'I don't think so, Emma.'

'Why not?'

'Her family mightn't want to be split up. Or they could have made their own arrangements.'

'But if they haven't? Could we go and ask?'

Dad shook his head at once. 'No, it's much too dangerous. The Falls area is a battle zone, Emma, no one goes there who doesn't have to. I'm sorry, love.'

'So what can we do?'

'We can only hope and pray that Maeve is all right. But the best thing I can actually do is my job. I'm telling the world the truth of what's happening here, and I hope that helps end it.'

Just then Mom came down the stairs in her nightgown. 'David,' she said. 'You look exhausted, honey.'

'I'm OK.'

Emma left her mother to fuss over Dad, and thought again about Maeve. Everything Dad had said sounded reasonable. So why did she still feel like she was letting down her friend, by being safe while Maeve was in danger?

'Please, Da.' said Sammy, sitting at the kitchen table. 'Please, don't go back out.'

It was breakfast time and Sammy had heard on the radio about the death the previous night of a nine-year-old boy in Divis Street, shot in his bed by a machine-gun bullet during a night of ferocious rioting. Sammy had listened with horror to reports of Catholics being burned out of their homes at Divis Street, and of how two-thirds of the houses on Conway Street had been set ablaze. Homes and businesses had also been torched in Dover Street, Percy Street, and Beverly Street, and the nationalist Ardoyne area was completely surrounded by loyalists. And now his father was finishing breakfast and about to take to the streets again, having boasted that he 'did his bit' during the conflict last night.

'Why wouldn't I go back out?' said Da as he pushed away his plate.

Sammy had to tread carefully. Earlier he had heard Ma trying to reason with his father, who simply overruled her objections to his involvement in street violence. Ma was in the bathroom now, and his sisters were still in bed, so Sammy had to take this chance to sway his father.

'We were all really worried about you last night, Da,' he said.

'Don't you worry; I'm well able to look after myself. Or do you think I'm not?' he asked challengingly.

'No, Da, it's not that.'

'Then you've no need to worry.'

'But Da, it's not good, it's–'

'What's not good?'

'Burning people's houses. A boy of nine was killed in his bed.'

'I'm sorry about the wain being killed, but this is war, Sammy.'

'Burning families out of their homes?'

'Do you think they wouldn't do it to us? Do you think the IRA have any qualms about petrol-bombing police stations?'

'But that doesn't make it right, Da.'

'It has to be done. They want our jobs, Sammy, they want our houses, they want this city!'

Sammy tried to think up a response, but his father ploughed on.

'These Fenians are rising up. It's armed revolution, son, and we've got to stop them. We're British men and women. We won't be ruled by Dublin, or the Pope in Rome!'

'But if it's really a rebellion, isn't that a job for the army and the police?

'The army are in their barracks. And the police can't cope. They're having to retreat to their stations, just to defend them.'

'But burning down–'

'Stop spouting that like a parrot!' snapped Da. 'We have to send them a message. We have to show them this is our country. And if that means burning every street off the Falls Road to the ground, that's what we'll do!'

Sammy was horrified and he decided to throw caution to the wind. 'Da, I've a friend who lives there.'

'What?!'

'Her name is Maeve Kennedy; she's a good friend of Dylan's sister. Her family are nice people; Ma met them at the art exhibition. They've nothing to do with the IRA; it can't be right to attack families like that.'

'I've told you already, this is war. You can't be friends with people from the other side.'

'Why not?'

'Because they're the enemy. It doesn't matter how nice they seem, they want to destroy our way of life and they're the enemy.'

'No, Da, it's … it's not that simple.'

'It is! You can't be friends with Taigs, get that into your skull. You're on one side or the other, there's no in-between.' Da rose from the table and pushed the chair roughly back. 'I'm going out to play my part. And I never, ever, want to hear you talking like this again.'

Sammy sat unmoving as his father left the house, and he gripped the edge of the table, forcing himself not to cry as the tears welled up in his eyes.

CHAPTER TWENTY-ONE

Maeve's heart sank as she listened to the kitchen radio. The news from across Belfast was bad. She had hoped that the rioting would die down, but instead it was spreading and becoming even bloodier.

Last night Aunt Nan had been trapped in the Ardoyne district where she had gone to visit a sick friend, and Maeve had spent a terrifying night alone in the house. Her aunt had rung a neighbour on Bombay Street and got a message to Maeve explaining her predicament. The neighbour had offered to let Maeve stay in her house, but Maeve felt she was too old to be babysat and instead had locked herself into her own home. Gunfire and petrol bombing, accompanied by screaming and shouting, had gone on long into the night and it was very late before Maeve finally fell into a fitful sleep.

She had been praying that Aunt Nan would get home this morning, but the new day hadn't brought any let-up, and local people were now battling it out on the streets with marauding loyalists.

Maeve tried to filter out the noise of fighting and explosions as she listened to the news on the radio. The newsreader painted a picture of a city out of control, but Maeve's heart started racing when he announced that two people had been killed in the

Ardoyne district. The report described the police coming under attack and responding with machine-gun fire that resulted in two civilian deaths. Maeve felt her mouth go dry. Please God, she thought, let it not be Aunt Nan!

Just then there was a loud bang nearby that Maeve suspected might be a car's petrol tank exploding. She quickly brought her ear right up to the radio, desperate to know who the victims in Ardoyne were. A burst of gunfire rang out in the distance and Maeve had to strain to hear the radio. Her heart was pounding, then the firing stopped and she heard the newsreader clearly. He said that the victims of the shooting were two young men in their twenties, and Maeve experienced a flood of relief. No sooner did she experience it than she felt guilty. Two people were dead, and it would be a tragedy for their families, yet she couldn't help but be relieved that it wasn't Aunt Nan. She thought of her aunt, whose charitable nature had resulted in her being trapped in Ardoyne, and she wished that she were here now. Even in a situation as bad as this, Aunt Nan would know what to do. But Aunt Nan wasn't here, nor was Uncle Jim or her father. She had chosen not to impose herself on neighbours, so she was on her own, and she felt a sudden stab of loneliness mixed with fear. Tears were welling up in her eyes, but she took a deep breath and steadied herself. Aunt Nan would get back as soon as was humanly possible. Meanwhile she needed to be brave and to weather the storm. Taking more deep breaths, she sat at the table, trying to make a plan that would keep her safe.

'Come on, Dylan,' said Mom, 'I'm worried sick about Dad. I can't take responsibility for Maeve as well.'

It was Friday afternoon now, and Dylan's father had left early that morning to cover the battlefield into which so many parts of Belfast had turned. Emma had failed to persuade Dad to rescue Maeve from her home at the frontline, and now Dylan was sitting in the drawing room with his mother, trying to get round her.

'Dad will be fine,' he said. 'He's a journalist; people know he's just reporting.'

'This isn't a normal war, Dylan. There are thugs on both sides rioting for the sake of it. People like that could turn on a journalist.'

'Dad's smart, he'd know when to walk away. But Maeve has never known anything like this. And she's on her own with her aunt. We can't just turn our backs if there's a chance of getting them out.'

'What we can't do, Dylan, is go into a war zone. I'm sorry, but my duty is to my own family.'

'We don't have to involve the whole family. If you just drove me nearby, I could run in to Bombay Street, find out if Maeve is all right, and run out again. And if it's really a battlefield and I can't get near, then OK, we turn back. But at least we'd have tried.'

'Dylan … you've a really good heart, and I'm proud that you're so loyal and caring about a friend. But I'm sorry, I can't take that risk. This is not our fight.'

Dylan was taken aback. 'It's not our fight? So we don't care what happens?'

'Of course we care. I've done everything I could for community spirit here. I exposed you and Emma to both traditions. I encouraged you to make friends from both sides of the divide. I invited Catholics and Protestants to my exhibition.'

'Yes, but—'

'But I'm your mother, and I'm responsible for you. So I'm sorry. But there's no question of risking your life. And that's final.'

Mom rose and walked out of the room, and Dylan stood staring into space, not knowing what to do next.

Sammy tried not to let his anger with Da show. It was late afternoon, and his father had come back to the house, full of his own importance, and boasting of how he and 'the lads' had played their part in the battles raging between loyalists and nationalists. Ma hadn't been able to get to work in the mill because of all the fighting, and she had tried to persuade Da not to become involved further in trouble, but he had blithely ignored her.

Now he slurped his plate of stew as he sat at the kitchen table.

'Nice stew, Rose,' he said, 'and by God, Taig-bashing gives you an appetite!'

'No good will come of that, Bill,' complained Ma, 'no good at all.'

'Enough of your wittering, woman!' said Da, and he dipped a slice of bread into his bowl to mop up the last of the stew. 'That was lovely,' he said. 'Almost as lovely as seeing the Taigs fleeing – and their houses going up in smoke!' he added with a laugh. He looked at Sammy as though expecting him to join in, but Sammy stared back, stony-faced. How could Da think there was something to laugh at in any of this?

Suddenly Da's face darkened and he stared at Sammy. 'What's wrong with you, sonny? You look like you've sucked a lemon!'

'I don't like what you're doing, Da,' answered Sammy quietly.

'You don't like what I'm doing?! Since when do I need you to like what I'm doing?!'

Sammy recognised the warning signs of his father's rising temper, but he couldn't bring himself to humour him today. 'What happens if my friend is in one of the houses that's burnt down?' he asked.

'Your friend? Some little Taig bitch!

'Bill,' said Ma sharply. 'That's uncalled for.'

'Don't tell me what's called for. What sort of a traitor have we reared?'

'I'm no traitor,' said Sammy. 'I'm for England and the Queen. But I don't have to hate everyone who's a Catholic, or a Jew, or different to us.'

'This is all tripe you've been fed by those bloody Goldmans. I should never have let them near the place!'

'I don't need the Goldmans to know right from wrong, Da.'

'You need to know where you stand, boy! I told you that this morning.'

'You can't be friends with somebody one minute and not care what happens them the next.'

'You can if I say you can!' said Da, rising from the table.

'No, Bill, please,' said Ma.

Sammy forced himself to stand his ground, still half expecting a blow despite Ma's plea. Instead his father stopped and looked at him calculatedly. 'Where does this girl live?' he asked.

'Bombay Street,' answered Sammy, puzzled at this change in direction.

'Good.'

'How do you mean?'

'Loads of trouble up there. She's probably already been burnt out of it, or fled to Andersonstown like the rest of the Taigs!'

'No!' cried Sammy.

'So put her out of your head.'

'She's my friend. I won't just abandon her'

'What are you going to do?' said Da sneeringly 'Ride to the rescue on a white horse?'

Da was being horrible and sarcastic, but his words made Sammy think. Maybe he could rescue Maeve if she was still in Bombay Street. What his father had been doing was wrong – but perhaps he could offset that by doing something right. It would be frightening to cross over into the nationalist Falls Road, and dangerous now that the area was a battleground, but he couldn't bear to think of something happening to Maeve while he stayed home and did nothing.

'Thanks, Da,' he said. 'You've made my mind up!'

'What?!'

'No, Sammy!' said Ma.

'I have to!' he answered. He made to run out before they could stop him, but something caused him to pause. There could be bullets and petrol bombs flying where he was going, so just in case anything happened he reached out and squeezed his mother's arm. He kissed her quickly on the cheek, then he turned on his heel and ran out the front door.

Maeve fought hard to keep panic at bay. She had been sitting in the kitchen, hoping that Aunt Nan might suddenly appear, or that the radio newsreader would report that the situation was calming down. Instead she heard the screaming and shouting from the nearby streets increasing in volume. Local men and youths had been manning makeshift barricades to try to keep out loyalist mobs that were causing havoc in the beleaguered streets of nationalist west Belfast. Maeve suddenly heard a loud guttural roar. It had an animal-like quality, and she feared that the barricades had been breached and that this was the sound of the mob pouring through. She had locked the doors and windows but that wouldn't delay for long any attackers determined to break into the house. Her mouth went dry and she found it hard to swallow. She tried breathing deeply but the sound of the roaring crowd was growing nearer. Maeve wasn't as religious as Aunt Nan or Uncle Jim but she made the sign of the Cross, bowed her head, and began to pray.

Sammy ran down Ebor Street, turned right and sprinted past the terraced houses along Broadway. He was safely on the loyalist side of the divide here, but his mind was racing. What would happen when he got to the flashpoint where the loyalist and nationalist areas merged? And how was he going to find his way past the barricades that had been erected around the streets off the Falls Road? His heart pounded, but he was fit from playing soccer and he settled into a steady pace. The further he got along the road the louder the sound of gunshots and explosions became. Men were on the streets, armed with pickaxe handles, rocks and petrol bombs, and there was an air of chaos as he reached the point where the loyalist area ended and gave way to a nationalist zone. Sammy could hear shouts from where fighting was raging nearby, but a plan was forming in his mind.

'Back you go, sonny!' cried a heavy-set man who was blocking the way. He was carrying a sharpened pole, and seemed to be the leader of a group of men who were arming themselves with clubs and rocks.

'I have to get to the hospital!' cried Sammy without breaking stride, 'my ma is injured!' The grounds of the nearby Royal

Victoria Hospital stretched back all the way to the Falls Road, and Sammy's impromptu plan was to make it to the hospital, find a way through its grounds and emerge out onto the Falls Road.

Sammy saw the heavyset man hesitate and, seizing his opportunity, he did a quick side-step and ran around him. He heard the man shouting after him but he sprinted as fast as he could and didn't look back. After a while Sammy had to slow a little, his chest tightening. The air was thick with smoke from burning cars and houses, and he saw vicious fighting going on at the bottom of a nearby side street. This was the frontline, and he felt his stomach tighten in fear. But if he hesitated he might lose his nerve altogether, and then what might happen to Maeve? He steeled himself, put his head down, and ran steadily ahead.

The sound of shooting grew louder and Maeve quickly finished praying and blessed herself. Normally her prayers were for Dad's safety in Cyprus, but today she had prayed fervently for Aunt Nan and herself. It took an emergency like this to bring home to her just how important her family was, and she wondered how the rioting mobs that were burning down family homes could live with themselves. Surely they too had families, mothers and fathers, brothers and sisters? How could they not see that the people whose homes they destroyed were just like them?

She heard a loud explosion from nearby and realised that it was time to stop reflecting and to act. Earlier she had made preparations in case the house was set ablaze. Following the lead of the heroine in an adventure book she had read, she had set up a wet blanket and buckets of water in her hiding place under the stairs. Time to go there now, she thought. She left the kitchen and opened the door leading under the stairs, then hesitated. Now that the moment had come she wasn't so sure this was the right move. The idea of going outside was terrifying, what with gunfire, petrol bombs and the clamouring mobs that she could clearly hear. But the hiding place under the stairs suddenly seemed very claustrophobic, and she hated the idea of being enclosed there like a trapped rat.

Her heart was pounding, and she felt perspiration forming on her forehead as she stood, terrified, at the doorway under the stairs, uncertain what to do.

☣ ☣ ☣

'Will you take a risk?' asked Emma, as she sat with Dylan in the sunlit dining room of their house. Even in the leafy suburb of the Malone Road, the distant sound of gunfire could be heard from town, and Mom had made them stay at home all day.

'What sort of risk?' said Dylan.

'I'm going to try and reach Maeve. Will you come with me?'

'Mom would have a fit!'

'She needn't know.' Emma could see that Dylan was uncertain, and she tried to speak convincingly. 'Look, you said it yourself to Dad. If we really can't get through we turn back, but at least we'll have tried. And if we do get through and Maeve is trapped, we get her in the car and bring her here. It could save her life.'

'What car are you talking about?'

'Mom's car. We'd have to take it.'

She could see that Dylan was shocked, but she ploughed ahead. 'It's an automatic, so one of us could drive it and the other could try to find the way through to Bombay Street. What do you say?'

Her brother didn't answer at once, and Emma looked him directly in the eye. 'She's our friend, Dylan. We'd never forgive ourselves if something happened to her.'

Dylan weighed it up, then he nodded. 'OK. Let's take Mom's car and go get her.'

'Are you out of your mind?'

Emma turned round in shock to find that her mother had entered the room.

'I can't believe you'd do this!' said Mom angrily.

'It wasn't Dylan's idea, Mom, it was mine,' admitted Emma.

'I don't care whose idea it was! Dad and I have both forbidden you to get caught up in this madness. What part of that isn't clear?!'

'I'm sorry, Mom,' said Emma, 'but I don't understand how we can do nothing.'

'So you'd risk being killed, when you don't even know for sure that Maeve is still in Bombay Street? I'm locking the house up, neither of you is leaving here till this is over.'

Emma went to protest but her mother raised her hand. 'No more arguments, Emma! I really hope Maeve is all right – but you won't die finding out!'

Her mother walked out of the room, and Emma lowered her head in despair.

Sammy ran out of the Royal Victoria Hospital onto the Falls Road. This was hostile territory. He felt scared, but he needed to catch his breath before continuing towards Bombay Street. The air was heavy with smoke from flaming vehicles and there was a smell of burning rubber, but Sammy gulped the foul air into his heaving lungs. The hospital was busy, with injured people being ferried in from all directions, and nobody had stopped Sammy as he had cut through its grounds.

He would have liked to rest a little more, but every moment might count, and he started off again. He ran along the Falls Road, passing Dunville Park. He was becoming oblivious now to the chaos of a city at war. The noise level was deafening, the streets were strewn with rubble, windows were smashed, vehicles were ablaze and barricades had been hastily erected.

Sammy ignored the upheaval and kept moving. Maeve's street was behind the Clonard Monastery, and he ran in that direction, then came to a halt where a barricade blocked the road. Wild-eyed youths armed with baseball bats were manning the obstruction, and some of them were building it higher with sheets of wood, metal bed frames and anything else that was to hand. They were being instructed by an older man who raised a hand, stopping Sammy.

'Where do you think you're going?' he asked.

'Bombay Street.'

'Forget it. The Prods have broken through, it's murder up there!'

Sammy felt his stomach tighten. If anything had happened to Maeve it would be unbearable. 'I have to get there,' he said.

'Why?'

'I live there. I have to find my ma!'

Sammy had given the first answer that came into his head, and now the man looked at him appraisingly.

'You're from Bombay Street?'

'Yes!'

'What's the street behind it?'

Sammy had no idea, and while he tried to think up a response the man locked eyes with him.

'What are you, son, a wee spy sent by the Prods?'

'No!'

'We'll soon find out,' said the man, moving towards Sammy.

'Petrol bomb!' cried Sammy, swiftly raising his hands protectively to his head and face.

The older man instinctively followed suit, and while he curled up to save himself from the blast of the non-existent bomb, Sammy turned on his heel and sprinted flat out away from the barricade.

Maeve pulled the door firmly shut behind her. It was dark and cramped under the stairs, but the sound of the mob had grown frighteningly close, and in the end she had decided that she couldn't possibly go outside.

Now she sank back against the wall and curled up in the furthermost corner. She didn't know if the water and wet blanket would protect her enough if the place was set on fire. The house was built of bricks, though, and she hoped that even if the worst came to the worst and it was torched, the basic structure would stay standing and she could survive.

Unless the mob found her. If they broke in and discovered her hiding place there was no telling what would happen to her. But there was nothing she could do about that now. She had made her decision. She breathed out to try to calm herself, and crouched against the wall, waiting to see what would happen.

Dylan banged the dining room table in frustration. 'I feel so helpless!' he said.

'I know,' answered Emma. 'I've been thinking, though. Mom said we can't go looking for Maeve. But maybe we could get someone else to.'

'How? Who would we get?'

Emma indicated the telephone. 'We could ring the police.'

'But it said on the radio they've been retreating to their barracks to defend them.'

'Every policeman in Belfast can't be in a barracks. There must still be some out on the streets.'

'Even if there are,' said Dylan. 'What would we say to them?'

'That there's a twelve-year-old girl in danger in Bombay Street. Her uncle is away and her aunt can't protect her.'

'We're not absolutely sure Maeve's still there.'

'It's really unlikely she got out. And if she did, OK, the police would give out to us for wasting their time. But I don't care, we can't do nothing if she is trapped.'

Dylan thought for a moment. 'There are people in danger all over Belfast. We need a reason for the police to rescue Maeve.'

'Like what?'

'Supposing we said she'd a health problem? Like a bad heart?'

'But she'd tell them she hadn't.'

'So what? The city is in chaos, and there's been a mix up. But at that stage the police would be at her house, probably in a Land Rover or an armoured car. On their way back out of the Falls they could take Maeve and her aunt with them.'

Emma looked thoughtful. 'I don't know, Dylan …'

'I don't know either! But it might save her life. And it's better than doing nothing.'

'Yeah … yeah, you're right.'

'OK', said Dylan, moving briskly to the phone. 'Let's do it.'

Sammy watched in horror as a row of houses blazed furiously up ahead. After escaping at the barricade he had taken a route that brought him closer to the interface between the loyalist Shankill and the nationalist Falls. There was bloody hand-to-hand combat going on in these streets, and he had kept moving, eventually finding his way into the warren of back-to-back housing near the Clonard monastery. What he saw shocked him profoundly, with the triumphant loyalists burning and wrecking homes, while outnumbered nationalists fought rear-guard actions and tried to escape.

'Which one is Bombay Street?' asked Sammy of a man at the head of a group of loyalists armed with crowbars.

'You mean which one *was* Bombay Street?' said the man with a grin. 'That's it ahead – going up in flames!'

Sammy couldn't believe it. He wanted to scream, but if he did the men might think he was a Catholic. Instead he just nodded in reply, then looked disbelievingly as the row of houses blazed furiously. The air was punctured with rifle and machine-gun fire, and he wanted nothing more than to run home, away from the madness and hatred. But he had come this far, and Maeve might still be here. He hesitated for a second, the horrifying sounds ringing in his ears, then he plucked up his courage and ran forward towards the mayhem that was Bombay Street.

Maeve kicked open the door under the stairs and burst out into the blazing, smoke-filled living room. She had survived the looters breaking into her house, but her plan of sitting out the riot had had to be abandoned. The looters had departed after torching the house, and the heat and the smoke had driven Maeve from her hiding place. Despite having wrapped herself up with the wet blanket Maeve felt almost overcome now by the wall of heat that hit her in the living room. The furniture was burning fiercely, but even worse was the thick, acrid smoke that made it impossible to see, and that brought on a fit of harsh, painful coughing.

Maeve felt that she was going to faint. She pushed out her right hand from within the blanket and steadied herself against the wall. It was hot to the touch, and she had to pull her hand away, but at least she had stayed on her feet. If she fainted now she would be fatally overcome by the fumes, and she tried desperately to get her bearings so that she could make for the hall door. She was weakened by another fit of coughing, however, and with the swirling black smoke she couldn't see her way.

He throat felt cracked and her eyes stung horribly. She felt a rising sense of panic, and her stomach tightened in terror at the idea of burning to death. No! She thought, she mustn't give up.

If she couldn't see the hall door then she would have to feel her way along the walls. The walls might burn her hands but it was the only way. Steeling herself, she reached out again and stumbled forward, desperately trying to find the way to the door before she passed out.

'It's no good!' said Dylan hanging up the phone. 'The police aren't going to help us.'

'What's the point of an emergency number if they fob you off?!' snapped Emma. She felt angry, but she realised there was no point taking it out on her brother. 'Sorry, Dylan,' she said, forcing herself to be calm. 'What did they say?'

'Same as the last time. They've emergencies all over the city. They have to prioritise.'

'Saving a twelve-year-old should be a priority!'

'I know.'

Emma racked her brains. 'Supposing we forget about dialling 999? Instead we ring her local police station. Maybe they could send someone to get her.'

'It said on the radio that it's war up around the Falls. Maeve's local station is probably under siege.'

'We have to try something! If her local station can't help, we ring the next nearest one. We can't just give up.'

'You're right,' said Dylan, crossing the room to get the telephone directory. 'I'll start calling them.'

Emma watched as her brother quickly flicked through the telephone directory, seeking the listing for the police. Despite her brave words, she felt a rising sense of despair, and she bit her lip, trying to keep the gloom at bay. But deep down she sensed that the police wouldn't be coming to the rescue. The thought sent a chill up her spine, and she turned from Dylan and looked away. She had never believed in ghosts, or premonitions, but for no reason that she could explain, she suddenly felt a strong sense of dread.

Maeve stumbled out the hall door and collapsed onto the street. The air was acrid from burning houses and vehicles but nonetheless she gulped it into her lungs. Despite the wet blanket her hair was singed, and her hand was painfully blistered and burned, but Maeve didn't care. She was so relieved to have escaped the blazing front room that she couldn't think about anything else right now. She continued to gulp air into her aching lungs as her head began to clear. She still felt a bit woozy but she gingerly dropped the blanket, sat up, and looked around.

Bombay Street was like something from a nightmare. Along the street her neighbours' homes were on fire, and the roadway was like a battlefield, with bricks, bottles and other missiles scattered everywhere. Gunfire was still being exchanged nearby, and the mob that had set fire to the houses was milling about. Some of the men were armed with rifles, the rest carried clubs and iron bars.

She needed to get out of here quickly, but as she went to rise, a brick missed her head by inches. She turned around in shock to see a boy of about fourteen pointing at her. 'Wee Fenian bitch!' he cried, then he picked up another stone from the ground. This time he didn't throw it, however, but instead held it threateningly in his hand and started towards her. Terrified, Maeve struggled to get to her feet, but she still felt light-headed. The boy smiled maliciously, lightly tossing the stone from hand to hand as he made his way towards her.

Sammy ran past burning houses, sickened by what he saw. It seemed that the people around him were no longer individuals, but had instead become unthinking members of a blood-crazed mob. Explosions rent the air, machine gun and rifle fire added to the din, and everywhere was the roaring of flames and the searing heat from the blazing houses. Worst of all, though, was the sense that he had left it too late to save Maeve. Bombay Street was a war zone, and Maeve's side had obviously lost this battle. And then, incredibly, he saw her. She was grappling fiercely with a teenage boy. The boy had a rock in his hand and he was trying to club Maeve with it. Sammy felt a surge of fury and he ran forward. Maeve had gripped the boy's wrist and was putting up a good fight. The boy was bigger and stronger than her, and with a sudden jerk he freed the hand holding the rock. He swung back his arm to strike, but doubled up in pain as Sammy ploughed into him and punched him full force in the stomach. The boy spluttered, but Sammy rounded on him. It was as though this thuggish boy represented all the awful things that Sammy had seen today. He angrily drew back his left fist, then unleashed a powerful upper cut that sent the bigger boy sprawling backwards onto the ground. The boy lay there groaning, and Sammy turned to Maeve.

'Sammy!' she said disbelievingly.

'Are you OK?'

'Yeah, just a few burns. What are you doing here?'

'I heard what was happening. So I came to get you.'

'Across Belfast?

'Yeah.'

'Oh, Sammy!' said Maeve, 'You're a friend in a million!' She squeezed his arm gratefully, and in spite of everything he found himself grinning at her.

'You can thank me later. Can you run?'

'Yes'

'Is your aunt here?'

'No, she's up in Ardoyne.'

Sammy indicated a couple of club-wielding men who were walking towards them.

'Time to get out of here!'

'OK,' said Maeve, 'let's go!'

Maeve ran down Bombay Street with Sammy at her side. Despite the horror all around her she felt a sense of exhilaration that her friend had crossed a war-torn city to rescue her. She had so many questions that she wanted to ask him – to say nothing of thanking him properly for the huge risks that he had taken in coming here. But now wasn't the time, and they both ran on, aware that they were far from being safe. Gunfire was still echoing through the streets, petrol bombs were exploding and vehicles, shops and houses were still being destroyed.

Maeve ran instinctively towards the Falls Road. She had heard on the radio that there was fighting on the Falls as well, but at least it was the centre of the nationalist area, and the route there would take them in the opposite direction to the loyalist Shankill. Now they suddenly slowed, seeing a group of armed men coming out of one of the burning houses.

'This way, Sammy!' she called, aware that he wouldn't know the warren of streets as well as she did. She ran away from the men, trying to find a route that would avoid the roving mobs. She ran past a smouldering car whose tyres were on fire and reached a corner. She could hear Sammy several yards behind her, then she began to round the corner. Suddenly there was a massive blast. The car erupted as its petrol tank exploded, and the last thing Maeve saw was a blinding flash of light, then everything went black.

CHAPTER TWENTY-TWO

ylan and Emma walked down the hospital corridor in silence. All the words had been spoken now, and nothing could change the horror of the last few days. Belfast had finally calmed down, through a combination of exhaustion and the arrival on its streets of the British Army as peacekeepers. In the four days since the burning of Bombay Street the troops had imposed order, and had erected barbed wire barricades between loyalist and nationalist areas. When the cost was counted, it emerged that eight people had been killed in the rioting, over seven hundred were injured and more than five hundred homes and businesses had been destroyed.

The scale of the devastation was shocking, but Dylan hadn't been able to take it in. Instead the last few days had been a waking nightmare. Before now he hadn't known anyone who had died, much less had to go to the funeral of a friend. Yesterday though, he had watched in a daze, standing in the bright sunshine that bathed Belfast City Cemetery, as his friend who had died following the car explosion was laid to rest. It had been the saddest day of Dylan's life, and as he thought about it now he felt tears welling up in his eyes again.

He walked on down the polished hospital corridor, trying to hold in his emotions, but his mind was in turmoil. Sammy had died a hero, because he wouldn't leave Maeve to her fate in Bombay

Street, but that didn't make his death acceptable. Dylan felt angry when people had gone on about Sammy's bravery, and he had felt like standing up in the church and shouting that Sammy shouldn't have needed to be a hero. Why couldn't people admit that instead of it being heroic, it was obscene that Sammy had died because hate-fuelled adults were rioting?

He felt a tear rolling down his cheek now, and Emma halted. Dylan stopped too, and Emma looked at him, then tenderly dabbed his cheek, offering him her handkerchief.

'Thanks,' he said, drying his eyes. 'I'm sorry, Emma, I–'

'It's fine,' she said softly. 'Really, it's fine. But before we go in to Maeve, I want to say something.'

'Yeah?'

'It's … it's awful about Sammy. And I know he was your best friend. But we could have lost two friends. We could have lost them both, Dylan, and we didn't. That's the way we have to look at it. And if Maeve can be brave, so can we. OK?'

Dylan realised that Emma was right, and that they had to be strong for Maeve. He finished drying his eyes and gathered himself.

'OK?' repeated Emma gently.

'Yeah, OK.'

'Come on then,' said Emma, and they continued down the corridor, with Emma gripping a carrier bag containing grapes and Lucozade for her friend. They stopped outside the door of Maeve's hospital room, then Dylan knocked and they entered.

Maeve was sitting in the bed, propped up on pillows. Her burnt right arm was swathed in bandages, her face was purple with bruising, and she looked so sad. Dylan thought she might be regaining her strength, however, and she definitely appeared better than when they had visited her yesterday after the funeral. They all exchanged muted greetings, then Dylan and Emma sat in chairs beside Maeve's bed after giving her the grapes and the Lucozade.

'How are you today?' Dylan asked.

'I can't stop thinking about Sammy. I can't … I just can't believe he's gone.'

'I know,' said Emma. 'We're the same.'

'I couldn't sleep for ages last night. I never got to thank him properly. And I keep thinking that if he hadn't come for me he could still be alive.'

'It's not your fault, Maeve,' said Dylan, 'you didn't start the riots.'

'I know, but–'

'No buts,' said Emma gently. 'It was just bad timing, you got round the corner, and Sammy didn't. It was no-one's fault – well, except for the fools causing all the trouble.'

'Please, Maeve. Don't blame yourself, that makes no sense,' said Dylan. To his relief, he saw Maeve nodding.

'I know you're right,' she said. 'But it's hard.'

There was a brief pause, then Emma spoke. 'So, what do the doctors say about you going home?' she asked, in what Dylan saw was a discreet attempt to change the subject.

'They told Aunt Nan I might be able to go home after tomorrow.'

'That's great,' said Dylan.

'Except we don't actually have a home any more.'

'You could stay with us till you get sorted out,' suggested Emma, 'we've loads of room. Your aunt and uncle too.'

'Thanks, Emma,' said Maeve 'but we're leaving Belfast.'

'To go where?'

'The Irish government is setting up camps across the border for people who've lost their homes.'

'Really?' said Dylan, shocked at the idea of refugee camps in a country like Ireland.

'It will only be for a while. When Dad comes back from Cyprus we might live in Dublin.'

'Right,' said Emma sadly. 'Sounds like we're all going to be split up.'

'It's not that far,' said Maeve. 'You can both come and visit me.'

'We're not going to be here that much longer,' explained Dylan.

'Oh?'

'Mom says Dad has more than played his part here. That some-one else can do the reporting in future.'

'So where will you go?' asked Maeve.

Emma shrugged. 'I don't know. To Leeds to begin with. After that, maybe back to the States.'

'So we'll all be broken up,' said Maeve.

'Yeah,' answered Dylan. 'Though of course we'll still write to each other.'

'And we brought you a present,' said Emma, reaching once

more into the carrier bag. She took out a bulky brown package and left it on Maeve's bedside locker.

'What is it?'

'A souvenir of our time together. It's a miniature tape recorder, with the edited radio programme.'

Maeve looked taken aback. 'I'd forgotten all about that. Thanks, Emma, thanks, Dylan.'

'It, eh … it has the recording we did of Sammy,' said Emma.

'Oh God …' said Maeve.

Emma reached out and squeezed Maeve's uninjured arm. 'I know it'll be really sad to listen to that now, but it's still great to have a record of him.'

Maeve looked thoughtful, then nodded. 'Yeah, it is.'

'And you don't have to play it till … well, till you're ready,' said Dylan.

'No. I'll play it tonight.'

Dylan looked at her in surprise, but Maeve explained. 'Aunt Nan says when someone dies it's really sad, but you can't shut them out of your mind to save yourself from the sadness. She says that only makes it worse in the long run. So even if it makes you cry, you cherish their memory.'

Dylan was impressed and he nodded.

'And Aunt Nan says that when you're not sure what to do, ask yourself what would the dead person want you to do.'

'So what do you think Sammy would want us to do?' asked Emma.

'I'm not sure,' said Maeve. 'What do you think, Dylan? You were his best friend.'

Dylan considered for a moment. 'I think he'd want us to go on and have happy lives. Good lives, where we did something useful. He never got to follow his dream, so I'd say he'd like us to follow ours. And I think … I think he'd like us to remember him sometimes.'

'Why don't we make a promise?' said Maeve. 'Why don't we promise that we'll never forget him, and that every year on the day he died, no matter where we are, we'll stop and remember him?' She stretched out her uninjured arm on the bed, and turned her hand face up. 'I promise, I'll never forget Sammy,' she said, her voice breaking.

Emma laid her hand on top of Maeve's and, blinking back the tears, made her pledge. 'I promise, I'll never forget Sammy.'

Dylan swallowed hard and placed his hand on top of the other two. 'I promise, I'll never forget Sammy,' he said softly. Then he closed his eyes as all three of them gripped hands, and for the first time since his friend had been killed, he felt the beginnings of a sense of peace.

CHAPTER TWENTY-THREE

Maeve breathed a sign of relief as Uncle Jim's van pulled out the exit gate and she left the hospital behind. She had been treated well by the doctors and nurses, but she was glad to leave the place that would always remind her of the saddest days of her life. She sat in the back seat of the van, looking out the window on the city that had been her home for the last three years. Although some efforts had been made to clear up the streets, Belfast still looked like a war zone, with rubble and burnt out buildings on view as they drove along. Aunt Nan and Uncle Jim sat unspeaking in the front of the van, and Maeve knew it must be really strange for them to abandon their home with little more than the clothes on their backs.

They were driving south to the border this morning. The plan was to stay at Gormanston air base, in one of the refugee camps set up by the Irish government, and Maeve was struggling with mixed emotions. Part of her was worried about living in a refugee camp, even temporarily, yet part of her was relieved to leave behind the bitterness and hatred generated by the previous week's riots.

She looked out the window as Uncle Jim left the Falls behind and drove into the city centre, and towards the road that led to the south. It was only now as she left her own area that she realised how much destruction had been caused in the fighting. And for what?

It would be really easy to hate the people who had started the riots and caused Sammy's death, yet she knew instinctively that hatred would make her bitter and unhappy. There were bad people on both sides of the divide, but there were lots of good, decent people too. Sammy's mother was living proof of it, and Maeve had been deeply touched when Mrs Taylor had sent her flowers and a get-well note at the hospital, despite the fact that she must have been overcome with grief at her son's death. And then there was Sammy himself, who had crossed a city engulfed in violence, because his loyalty to a friend meant more than blind allegiance to his own tribe.

Maeve's thoughts were interrupted as her aunt indicated a signpost that showed the way to Dublin. 'Well, that's the end of us and Belfast,' said Aunt Nan quietly.

They were leaving the city, and Maeve turned around to take a last look. She had had good fun in Belfast, especially since becoming friends with the Goldmans and Sammy. Now, though, it would always be associated with sadness and the death of her friend. But while Sammy's death was heartbreaking, Maeve was determined that it would also inspire her anytime she doubted the basic goodness of human nature. She would keep forever the pledge she had made with Dylan and Emma, and she would never forget Sammy, the best friend she had ever known. Consoled by the thought, she sat back in her seat as the van left Belfast, then she looked ahead, ready for whatever the future might hold.

EPILOGUE

The Goldmans moved back to America. Emma went on to train as a journalist and had a successful career in radio and television. Specialising in music and entertainment, she made numerous award-winning documentaries. She settled in Washington where she became a noted middle distance runner, and nowadays she still competes in senior marathon races.

Dylan founded a big sports equipment company in New York. Every summer he organises the Wanderers Soccer Camp on Long Island, and on the final day he presents a cup called the Sammy Taylor Memorial Trophy.

Mrs Goldman continued to work as an artist and her work was exhibited in galleries in Dublin, Leeds, Boston and New York.

Mr Goldman remained an influential and respected journalist on both sides of the Atlantic and was highly regarded for his first-hand accounts of the early days of the Northern Ireland Troubles.

After Sammy's death his father ended all involvement with street violence and paramilitaries. He never got over his son being killed, however, and died of a heart attack the following year.

Sammy's mother emigrated to Canada with her remaining children. After several years she remarried happily, and with her new husband she opened a business importing Irish linen for distribution to shops across Ontario.

Gordon Elliot drifted out of football and into the illegal Ulster

Volunteer Force. He died at the age of twenty-two, when a bomb he was transporting exploded prematurely.

Mr Doyle and his family left Belfast after his home and shoe shop were burnt down. He moved to Cork, where he had relatives, opened another shop, and became involved again in training runners.

Buckie was shaken by Sammy's death and never boasted again about his days as a paratrooper or a special constable. After the B Specials were disbanded in August 1969 he concentrated all his spare time on coaching with Wanderers Football Club.

Maeve, Aunt Nan and Uncle Jim lived for a time in the refugee camp set up by the Irish government at Gormanston, County Meath. Maeve settled in Dublin with her father after he left the army. Aunt Nan and Uncle Jim settled in Dublin also, with Uncle Jim and Maeve's father setting up a company that made garden sheds. Maeve stayed involved with amateur running and went on to become a PE teacher. She married happily and had children, but every year she makes a journey, on her own, to Belfast, to lay flowers on the grave of her childhood friend, Sammy Taylor.

HISTORICAL NOTE

In the aftermath of August 1969 there was mass upheaval, with thousands of refugees from the conflict in Northern Ireland coming south of the border and staying in camps in the Republic of Ireland. By October 1971 approximately twelve thousand refugees had passed through Gormanston Camp in County Meath.

The conflict in Northern Ireland, widely known as 'The Troubles', claimed over three thousand lives and continued for almost thirty years. In 1997 the IRA called a ceasefire, and The Good Friday Agreement of 1998 paved the way for intensive negotiations that eventually led to the disbandment of the IRA, which was followed by the loyalist UDA and UVF also ending their armed campaigns. Both sides agreed to share power, with Northern Ireland governed from Stormont by a power-sharing executive.

Stormclouds is a work of fiction, and the families of Maeve, Sammy, Dylan and Emma are figments of my imagination. However, the historical elements from 1969 are real, with the bombing of the water reservoirs, the moon landing, and the burning of people from their homes all being actual events.

The Mourne Wall, visited during the picnic scene, is a real structure, still standing to this day. The wall passes over fifteen mountains, including Slieve Donard, the highest mountain in Ulster, and took eighteen years to complete.

Ardara Running Club and Wanderers Soccer Club are both fictitious, but Bombay Street, where Maeve lived, the Malone Road where the Goldmans rented the house and Ebor Street, where Sammy lived, are all actual places that still exist in Belfast, although they have changed since 1969.

Brian Gallagher
Dublin 2013

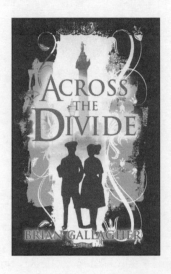

ACROSS THE DIVIDE

Liam and Nora form an unlikely friendship when he helps her out during a music competition. Liam's father, a mechanic, is a proud trade union member, while Nora's father is a prosperous wine importer. When Jim Larkin takes on the might of the employers in 1913, resulting in strikes, riots and lockouts, Liam and Nora's loyalties are torn and their friendship challenged.

A Boy. A Girl.
A Nation Torn Apart.

Taking
Sides

Brian Gallagher

TAKING SIDES

Annie Reilly wins a scholarship to Eccles Street School. There she makes friends with Susie O'Neill, and, through her, Peter Scanlon, a boy from a wealthy family who goes to school at Belvedere. But civil war is brewing in Ireland and hotheaded Peter has become involved in running messages for the rebels. When Annie is kidnapped, Peter is forced to make a terrible choice. Should he risk his life and betray his cause for Annie? And can they ever be friends again after this?

SECRETS AND SHADOWS

When her home is destroyed in the Luftwaffe bombing of the
North Strand, Dublin in 1941, Grace Ryan has to move to a different
part of the city. There she meets Barry Malone, sent to Ireland from
Liverpool to escape the air raids there. They both join a summer
sports club run by Barry's teacher, Mr Pawlek. However, they
begin to suspect Pawlek of spying for the Nazis. When Grace and
Barry attempt to find proof, an exciting challenge soon turns into
a highly dangerous mission, with their very lives at stake.